# EMOTIONAL ARITHMETIC

## MATT COHEN

# EMOTIONAL ARITHMETIC

## MATT COHEN

St. Martin's Press
New York

*For my children*

EMOTIONAL ARITHMETIC. Copyright © 1990 by Matt Cohen.
All rights reserved. Printed in the United States of America.
No part of this book may be used or reproduced in any
manner whatsoever without written permission except in
the case of brief quotations embodied in critical articles or
reviews. For information, address St. Martin's Press,
175 Fifth Avenue, New York, N.Y. 10010.

Library of Congress Cataloging-in-Publication Data

Cohen, Matt
    Emotional arithmetic / Matt Cohen.
      p.    cm.
    ISBN 0-312-13064-3
    I. Title.
  PR9199.3.C58E48   1995
  823'.54—dc20                   95-15832
                                               CIP

First published in Canada by Lester & Orpen Dennys Limited

First U.S. Edition: August 1995
10  9  8  7  6  5  4  3  2  1

I

## 1. That Afternoon, My Mother's Hands

It was July and that afternoon we were in the crystal blue heart of a perfect summer.

My mother's hands were in repose, spread out as if to be examined on the glass-topped table between us. Her long fingers were tipped with manicured pearl nails that floated on her skin like the moons of a faraway planet. The table, the chairs, my mother and I were all in the shade of a towering oak tree.

"I'll have a cigarette."

Suspended on the polished glass, aside from her cigarettes and lighter, was one of the bulging file folders she always carried. It was the old-fashioned kind, accordion bottom and scarlet ribbons at the top. Inside were her lists, her letters, her documents of imprisonment, betrayal and suffering. Glued to the front of the file was a white label reading, in capital letters, VICTIMS & PRISONERS.

I opened the cigarette package, offered it to my mother. And then, when she was ready, I stood to hold the flaming lighter in place. As she sucked on the filter her cheeks contracted into small knots of muscle and her unlined forehead furrowed with that familiar pattern of what I used to think was concentration and intelligence.

The gold lighter clicked loudly as I replaced it on the glass. Dangerous, some might say, for a mental institution. But this institution was different and in any case my mother, though she didn't know it, was soon to be released.

"Your father used to smoke. He gave me the lighter and the wedding ring at the same time. Look at the initials—MLW—the same on both of them."

My mother took off her ring—the gold wedding band was the only ring she wore—and held it out to me. "MLW. Do you remember what they stand for?"

"Melanie Lansing Winters," I said. With my mother, the essential thing was always to play the part.

"I used to have the Melanie Lansing School of Dance. Do you remember? That was before we moved to the farm. Of course I was better at singing. But no one wanted to send their children to singing school. They couldn't sit still for that. It was jump and twist and moan. It was dance, dance, dance. But I'll tell you the secret of the stage." She leaned forward. In those dancing-school days her hair was a rich chestnut colour that used to glow after she washed it. Now the dye that kept away the grey had made her hair a brittle and coppery red. But age had not destroyed her face. Only drawn the skin more tightly, squeezed out the softness, made her features sharper and more commanding than ever. Nor had the colour of her eyes changed. They were a sharp pulsing blue, always reminding that you were about to fail her.

"The secret of the stage, dance or no dance, is being still. Let the others jerk around like monkeys. They're only making fools of themselves. You stay up front, unmoving, the centre of the storm. Do that and all the eyes are on you. The Melanie Lansing School of Dance. I should have had the Melanie Dancing School of Lance. Did you ever think of that?"

"No."

"Your father would have helped me with that. Mrs. Dance and Mr. Lance. We could have been quite a pair, what do you think?"

"You *are* quite a pair."

2

"Only one problem. Mr. Lance had to go a-poking. Joking and moping and poking until he poked his way into someone else. Now what kind of school is that?"

Suddenly my mother's eyes switched modes: the lights went out and they began to fill. I wanted to lean over the table and take her hands in mine but I didn't. I waited. The tears began to roll down her cheeks but her eyes stayed open, fixed on mine. Then her mouth twisted, lips gripping each other like despairing hands.

"Madness," she croaked theatrically, "that way lies madness." She laughed, a sharp knowing laugh she had learned since her on-and-off separations from my father. Separations that started with her moving to a hotel or a neighbour's or a house or an apartment, but quickly developed into situations like the one we were in. Until finally for some reason—or perhaps just out of desperation—my parents recommenced their life together. As they were once more about to—this time because of an elderly man who was at more or less this moment packing his suitcases in some unimaginable Moscow apartment and preparing to come and spend the rest of his life with us, more specifically with his benefactress-to-be, my mother. Although, on the afternoon of which I speak, she was unaware of these developments because they were described in a letter that had not yet made its way into her file.

She took a tissue from her purse, wiped her eyes. "How is the old goat anyway?"

"Getting along."

"Goating along, you mean. Did you know he turned seventy-two last year? Seventy-two! When we got married everyone said he was too old for me. Now he's an old man and I'm—" My mother's face again began to ripple. She struggled to control it, like a pilot battling an aircraft that had gone into a tailspin. Sudden changes in pressure. Co-pilot unconscious. Just before the passengers have to bail out, the sky clears again and the pilot regains control, debonairly blowing smoke rings while a thin trickle of blood dries on his chin. The point of perfect stillness.

"Now he's an old man and I'm in an insane asylum for the rest of my life."

"You're not insane and you're not here for the rest of your life."

"Until—"

"Until the doctors say you're ready to leave. Any day now."

"I was the one who told your father to leave. You were away at college then. I waited for that. Then one morning at breakfast I read him the Riot Act. 'You're a pig and an idiot,' I told him. 'You should have declared moral bankruptcy ten years ago.' I said more than that, too, but I don't think he was even listening. I had wanted to hurt him but he was glad for the excuse. Anyway I sent him a present but he never wrote back. I don't think he knows what to make of me, do you? Do you?"

"No," I said. And it was true. That afternoon—like most others—I had no idea what to make of my mother. The best I could do was offer cigarettes, play my part.

"Your sister was smarter, she got away."

"She didn't get away. She was here last week."

"Once in six months. That girl is an expert on everywhere but her own home."

"She finds it difficult to see you because she loves you so much."

"Am I that bad?"

"No, you're not bad at all."

"When I go to heaven, you can be the judge."

My mother once said about my father—Professor Doctor David Winters, the eminent or at least emeritus historian—that he passed judgement the way other people passed wind. For her, with her files, her dossiers, her records of humanity's crimes, judgement was a matter of arithmetic. Emotional arithmetic. Like these visits, which were exercises in the emotional arithmetic of love and hate, time passed and time remaining, injustices suffered and revenge meted out. That afternoon, as always, my job was to be the objective witness, the recorder of my mother's sufferings, the messenger between my mother's pain and God's record book. My back had begun to ache and a sharp flame was burning in the pit of my stomach.

"You're looking great today," I finally said.

"What's the best thing about me?"

"Today? I'll tell you the best thing about you today." The momentum had shifted my way and now I could stare at my mother, who was suddenly squirming, shy and girlish, as though I were a judge torn between the triumphs of a hundred dazzling beauties.

"You're staring," she said. "No fair staring."

The flame in my stomach was beginning to sputter. If I could appease my mother it would go out. If, on the other hand, I could not manage her; if the bantering turned into accusations, the accusations into tears and rantings; if finally she went entirely out of control and I had to be rescued by the paid staff—then the flame would explode.

"I need to look at you. I can't decide with my eyes closed."

My mother smiled. The flame went out. One of the nurses was crossing the lawn towards us. Carefully, especially on that afternoon, I kept my eyes from shifting until she was finally ready to join the conversation.

"Mrs. Delfasco, what do you think is most attractive about my mother today?"

"Her hands," Julia Delfasco said right away. "Mrs. Winters, you have the most beautiful hands I've ever seen." There was a comfortable finality in her voice, the sound of a truth being pronounced, not for the first time.

Now I could stand up. "Not so fast," my mother said. "What about you?"

"Your tongue," I said. "I don't know what I'd do without your tongue." On that afternoon I was able to wink at my mother. As her smile came again, I leaned over and kissed her quickly on the cheek. Then, as always when things had gone well, I nodded without saying goodbye and in the same motion started on my way.

*2. Levin*

That afternoon, the afternoon it was decided my mother would be released, she had been at Heritage Acres for almost a year. The reason we had chosen such a place for her was simple: the chief psychiatrist was a man called Laurence Levin—old family friend, go-between in his own way, husband to my sister Ruth. Ruth was the travel writer, always somewhere else. But despite my mother's accusations, it was our father Ruth couldn't forgive.

I was the first to meet Levin. We were in a chemistry lab, learning to measure something disgusting with urine samples— I remember the yellow fluid in its glass containers. As always, I had my notebook in front of me. My own books of numbers were methodically kept: notes from class, results from the laboratory, readings from textbooks—I copied them all down carefully, hoping enough would rub off. A hockey player in medical school: I was always convinced that I had only been accepted because of my father.

Right away I could see that Levin was the kind of son my father must have had in mind. Dark, slight, quick. A North Toronto Jew who spoke with the accent I was sure I could hear in the voices of other rich Toronto Jews. I was in that part of the class marked off for possible failure, the almost dumb, well-rounded, well-intentioned boys and girls who had been low on marks but high on "character". The fodder. The reliable types who wouldn't get addicted to drugs or have sex with their patients.

Levin, on the other hand, was going to be a specialist. A researcher or a gynecologist or an explorer of some as-yet-unknown cellular mystery.

"Winters," Levin said, leaning over the desk and looking at the page where I was noting my results, "what the fuck are you doing?"

Meaning, I knew, that I was crazy to be writing down the results of the actual experiment when I could be using an equation to generate the right figures.

So I didn't answer. Smart guys like Levin, boys who had polished and hardened their Toronto accents while I had been hauled off to the country to learn about nature and cows—I didn't know how to be with them.

"Winters," said Levin, "I asked you a question."

"I'm looking at my piss and writing down my numbers."

"Thank you. Thank you for giving me an answer." Levin's voice was full of his self-confident Toronto sarcasm. But we weren't in Toronto. We were in Kingston, at medical school. Toronto was the big city where the rich Jewish boys came from, but Kingston was just a little town built on some big rocks.

It turned out I was right about Levin—to a certain extent. That is, he was Jewish, he was from Toronto, he was a smart guy hoping to be a specialist. But he had a weakness. "Tits," he informed me, the first time we got drunk together, "I'm going to specialize in tits and do you know why?"

"Because it's the only way you'll get to see them?"

"Wrong, Winters, or maybe right. But what you've missed is that the reason is philosophical. As Socrates says, a man with a handful of tits is not empty-handed."

"And you chose medicine over philosophy?"

"Okay, Winters, I'll tell you the truth. Since I can see you're a perceptive fellow. Appearances notwithstanding. I'll tell you why. You see in me a man who worships women. Despite all the warnings my mother gave me, I fall in love twenty times a day. Even here. And I am not talking carnal love. Nor philosophical love. When I sit on a bus and see an unintentionally exposed bit of leg, when a happily married library worker turns her face up to me at her desk, when I look across the street even in mid-winter and notice that little dot of colour on the cheek of a member of the fairer sex—I die."

"Levin, you need to get fucked."

"How crude you are. But I expected that. No, Winters, sex will not cure me—it only distracts. What I am looking for is total unceasing full-body contact, twenty-four hours a day."

"Professional help?"

"That's a better idea. But on the other hand, expensive. Why not, on the third hand, be the professional myself and let my clients help me?"

Typical, in other words. But shortly after I met Levin, my father got what he'd always wanted: an appointment as full professor in the Department of History at the University of Toronto. He bought a house there and managed to persuade my mother to stay at the farm with Ruth while she finished high school. I moved into a conveniently empty bedroom in Levin's apartment.

"The Nazis are coming!" Levin would scream, barging into my room in the middle of the night—drunk, wired on pills, triumphant or struck down in his latest attempt to penetrate the female psyche. "Gestapo visit, give me your papers or die the death of Canadian wine!" At which he would produce a bottle of dark purple tongue-staining poison and I and my own love of the moment would slide from sheet-clutching panic to a night-long session of cigarettes, booze, Levin's accelerating rant.

And meanwhile Levin was stuffing me with what I needed: little bits of information about the human body, anatomical details, explanations of biological theories, chemistry, physics, pharmaceutics—to me the contents of our courses made up an unconnected welter of details I could only hope to partially absorb; but to Levin they were all of a pattern, a pattern he'd easily glimpsed, a pattern I never exactly saw myself but which Levin must have wedged into my unconscious, because after I moved in with Levin, passing my exams was never a problem.

It turned out our whole family had an affinity for Levin. My mother was the next to meet him. On the big day, when I came from hockey practice to pick Levin up for the drive home, he was wearing a white shirt and a dark suit. He had shaved. He looked as though he were going to a funeral. When we got to the farm Levin made a bee-line for the house, barged in on my mother, drew his chair beside hers, starting talking; they shot off together like little toy race cars and all I could do was keep them supplied with coffee. Before the afternoon was over my mother had taken out her files. No problem for Levin. He slid into her world of prisoners, refugees, letters to heads of state, as though it were the womb he himself had emerged from.

She even showed him her own book of numbers. He wept with her as her fingers swept down the columns showing how many Jews were shipped each week from Drancy to Auschwitz. He held onto the photograph of her as a child—picking her out right away without hints—so tightly that he kept having to put down his coffee cup in order to smoke.

When my sister Ruth arrived home on the bus she took one look at Levin, then attached herself to him like an orphan puppy to a bitch. In awe, admiring—God knows why—but I have to admit Levin was clever enough to realize from the beginning that this odd-looking high school student was probably the only female who would ever tolerate him.

Even my father eventually succumbed. "My son," he said to Levin, shaking his hand and welcoming him into the family on the day of the wedding. And Levin, the tux boxed starchily around his scrawny frame, just a bit taller than my father, was equal to the occasion. "Dad," he said, giving my father a sinewy hug that left them both blushing.

## 3. Daytime Stars

On my way to Levin's office I passed Norton Meredith, co-owner and chief physician of Heritage Acres, sitting behind his desk. His window was open to the perfect afternoon. Perfect, also, was the view from his opened windows across the lawn to where my mother and Julia Delfasco now sat drinking tea. Had Meredith been spying on our little drama? Put it this way: everything about Meredith dared you to dislike him. "I called this place Heritage Acres," Meredith explained to me the first time I came, "because so many of our guests dream about times past." Today Meredith was a dream that began with coiffed white hair set in a gel smelling of test-tube flowers, continued with a designer polo shirt with one too many undone buttons, climaxed in his carefully tended naked sandalled feet propped up on the window-sill.

"Better today?" Meredith's smooth and indifferent voice gave off the same message as his appearance. And yet when he spoke he always leaned forward—smiling, earnest. "I give myself to my patients," he had told me.

Before Heritage Acres my mother had tried other, more conventional hospitals. Hospitals in Kingston and downtown Toronto. Doctors in three-piece suits who didn't wear sandals and who kept their feet on the floor. To begin with they had pre-scribed group therapy and tranquillizers. Eventually it became a matter of round-the-clock sedation, screaming confrontations, suicide attempts, until finally during one visit I was told my mother was being "placed in restraining garments for her own protection".

Now she was at Heritage Acres. "What we have here," Norton Meredith had explained, "is a unique institution and environment. I can promise you only three things: it will be ex-pensive, we will surround your mother with an alternative to her current life, we won't lie to you."

Like its owner, Heritage Acres was dressed for the occasion. Antique pine beds, tables, armoires. Money in the colour of wood. Across from Meredith's desk was a bookcase in the Heritage Acres style. The golden pine was scarred and cracked as though it had met Father Time in a back alley. "What do you think?" Meredith now asked, seeing me looking at his treasure.

"Nice." No point mentioning I had once had a summer job working for a carpenter who made "antiques" out of old barnboard; it had been my job to attack the wood with hammers and greasy bicycle chains.

"I'm glad you like it." Meredith stood up. He was tall and thin. When I used to play hockey, he was the kind of person I was careful not to hurt if he was on the other team, the kind of person I had to protect if he was on my own. "I hear your mother may be leaving us."

I nodded.

"You realize," Meredith said, "that as your mother, and as your father's wife, Melanie Winters hardly exists any more. If you take her out of here and try to put her back into her former situation—that of mother and wife—you'll be back to the suicidal and schizophrenic woman you started with. This time ten years older. This time with her reserves exhausted. This time bitter that she has lost not only her first family but her situation here, which is the best thing she has been able to manage since."

From Meredith's window I could see that my mother had now linked arms with her nurse and was walking around the lush expanse of manicured lawns, fertile flower beds and carefully tended trees that was Heritage Acres. In an ironic way this hospital *was* what my mother had always wanted: it was the farm brought to civilized perfection, nature under control, nature blooming to delight the senses without offending.

"You're threatening me?"

"I'm reminding you that people change. 'What happened to the human being I used to know?' people ask. 'Where did my mother go? My father? My husband? My child?' They think the previous person is hiding somewhere in the sick person. But it's not true. The previous person went on a one-way trip to become the sick person. And even if the sick person becomes well, the mother or father or child you used to know never comes back.

"What I'm trying to tell you is that your mother is in a new world. A world in which she has a secure place, a world in which she can survive in comfort, a world which does not punish her when she has a crisis. This is the world she prefers now. This is the only world she can live in. If you like, she's no longer your mother—anyone's mother—she's a child in a family devoted to her happiness. If she were to leave here and move back to Toronto or even to the farm, in six months—"

Meredith sat down at his desk again. "What about your father?" he suddenly asked. "How does he feel about this?"

"It's a joint decision," I said, although I knew my father was far from calm about the prospect of Melanie on the loose; of Melanie turning up at his office and breaking into tears in front of the students; of Melanie driving up to the Toronto house in the middle of the night and leaning on the horn until my father had to hide his student in the closet or wherever, then come down to bargain in front of the whole neighbourhood.

All these things had happened, plus more and worse. But those were the years when my parents separated and reunited with embarrassing regularity. The years during which rejection transformed Melanie Lansing Winters, the once obedient mother and housewife, into an infinitely resourceful and energetic shrew.

At first I had even found these incidents funny, and laughed with her over the public humiliations she had forced upon my father. Then came the phone call at four in the morning.

"This is operative fifty-four," a thick voice announced.

"Wrong number," I said, not recognizing my mother's voice. Nor did I recognize it when she kept on: "Benjamin, this is operative *fifty-four*. You are being called into service, Benjamin, the free ride is over. Meet me down at City Hall in thirty minutes for further instructions."

I hung up and went back to bed. Half an hour later the phone rang again. This time my mother didn't bother to disguise her voice; she was crying and screaming that no one had remembered her birthday. When I got to her she was dramatically splayed out on the couch she had bought with the settlement from the first of several legal separations. All of which led to reconciliations that my father duly telephoned me to announce—"Benjamin, I'm delighted to inform you, again, that your parents have once more renewed their conjugal bonds" was the formula he finally arrived at.

Semi-conscious, head rolling loosely from shoulder to shoulder, she pointed to the floor. As though I might otherwise miss seeing the proverbial dead soldiers—three empty pill bottles and two empty bottles of whisky. How much she had really swallowed or drunk I didn't even try to find out. I called the ambulance and we went to the hospital. The hour with the stomach pump must have been extremely unpleasant—she never attempted or threatened suicide again.

' Meanwhile, Norton Meredith was waiting. If I wanted to sit in silence remembering my mother's disasters, if I wanted to discuss my mother's departure, my parents in general, financial arrangements—even if I wanted, psychologically speaking or perhaps otherwise, to drop my pants—it was all, the expression said, the same to him. The meter was running, the taxi of mental health was en route, he was the chauffeur and I the passenger: all that remained was for me to name the destination. He was at my service—Norton Meredith: doctor, entrepreneur, custodian of the wandering spirit. I, on the other hand, was not a doctor. After I had "resigned" in the middle of my first year of internship—in, as a matter of fact, the field of psychiatry—I had been granted an indefinite leave of absence. To cure myself. Or at least to let time knit, etc.

On Meredith's desk was a copy of the letter that had forced our decision to allow my mother out of the hospital.

Moscow, June 15, 1989

Dear Melanie,
To my surprise, my request for a visa has been granted.
    In front of me I have the official document itself. As I told you previously, Zev has decided to go to Israel. He has offered to take me with him and continue to care for me there. But he is young enough to start again. Even to marry again. I hope he does: I feel that his generosity towards me has interfered with his own life long enough. I do not want to burden his future. If, therefore, you still truly wish to have me, I am yours.
    I must tell you I am not the man you remember. I am old. But my health is not too bad. If your offer still stands I propose to come to Canada as soon as I have organized my things and helped Zev to clear out the apartment. To divide the trip, and perhaps assure my arrival in good condition, I will stop in Paris for a couple of days to see Christopher. By the time you see me I will be used to being an émigré once more.
    Yours
    Jakob

Meredith now pointed to the letter. "This would be the man she's spoken about with Doctor Levin? And she and your father would care for him?"

"Yes. On the farm for the summer and then, when Jakob is ready, in Toronto. Why not? As you say, she can't go backwards, but perhaps with Jakob she'll find another way—"

To my surprise Meredith was nodding enthusiastically. Then he was pacing excitedly in his office, explaining to me how this really *could* give new life to my mother, that all these years she had been like a one-legged creature, hopping about in search of her second leg—which Jakob Bronski, the unexpected apparition from her past, would now provide. "The crazy leading the weak, yes, but surely that's what we *need*."

He sprang up to shake my hand. "Until next time." And then, as I was walking down the hall, I was sure I could hear a mocking "Good luck" drifting along behind me.

Levin, too, was sitting behind his desk. And his office, too, had a view onto the lawn of Heritage Acres. And though his windows weren't French, just aluminum colonial imitations that cranked open with a metal gizmo, Levin might also have been watching and overhearing the little conversation on the lawn.

As I came into his office, Levin was fanning himself with his own copy of Bronski's letter, the passport that was going to spring my mother from Heritage Acres. Or Stalag Estomac, as she had renamed it—in tribute to the food, which she detested.

"Your mother and I have been talking about daytime stars." He paused, a rhetorical Levin-like pause. "Do daytime stars mean anything to you?"

"Soap operas?"

"Exactly," Levin said complacently. "You're like all the others, as your mother was telling me. No one ever thinks about the stars in the daytime. At night, sure—even the most insensitive lout likes to gaze up at the sky and spout platitudes about those twinkling little orbs. But let the world turn, let the sun's light make them invisible—and bang—they're out of sight, out of mind until the next clear evening when you've had a few too many drinks and stumble outside...."

"Good point." I sat down.

"Dr. Winters, I think you have failed to grasp the implication of daytime stars."

"Enlighten me, Dr. Freud."

"The point is, Dr. Winters, the point your mother has grasped, is that those stars influence us even when they are invisible."

"Yes?"

15

"And yet, Dr. Winters, we cannot even see them. Cannot even see what constellations they belong to. Perhaps, even, sets of stars entirely unknown to us shine invisibly during the day."

"And?"

"Influence us, my dear Winters. Guide and shape our destinies with their invisible rays, their magical magnetic fields. Rays and fields no less strong, no less powerful, no less real than those from the stars we see—"

"Dr. Levin, once again I formally accuse you of conspiring to keep my mother in a state of insanity."

"Your mother and I have an understanding. 'Laurence,' she told me, 'to succeed in life you must lead with your mind.' Have you ever considered, Dr. Winters, the beneficial possibilities of leading with the mind?"

And now Levin, old friend, brother-in-law, unstable comic-opera psychiatrist who, due to losing all his money with a broker he had foolishly trusted, had needed to accept Norton Meredith's offer of employment at Stalag Estomac, jumped up from his desk and peered out his window, forcing me to follow, so we could together look at my mother and Julia Delfasco huddled together over that portion of the rock garden they had planted a few months ago.

My mother was kneeling at the flowerbed, pulling at something. She motioned to Julia. Julia was wearing shorts; when she bent to inspect what my mother wanted to show her, the curve of her bottom, the smooth line of her tanned legs, floated across the lawn like a perfectly formed question mark.

"She has the touch," Levin said.

When I met Levin he was scrawny and black-haired. Now his black hair was a salt-and-pepper wedge and the flesh around his eyes had the crumpled look of old snow. "She's dried him up," my mother complained once, when she was angry at Ruth. "She's a barren old stick and she's using him for a pisshole."

Levin had married Ruth nine years ago. Same year, same month, as Helen and I. We even talked about taking our honeymoons together. But it was only a joke: Helen and I were struggling, but Levin was already rich on his father's money, a clever young intern riding the market on margin into a dazzling sunset of big mortgages, sports cars and semi-annual trips to Europe.

"You got the itch?" Levin now asked.

"Do you?"

"You're avoiding, Dr. Winters."

## 4. Meanwhile, My Father: Part I

"When I die you'll know how lucky you were," my father used to tell me, my father Doctor Professor David Winters. That was when he taught Canadian history at Queen's University in Kingston, a half-hour drive from the farm.

My school also took a half hour to reach. I would walk from the house down the lane to the dirt road where I would stand beside the mailbox and wait for the school bus. Dreading it, at first, when I was still a city boy forcibly transplanted. "Your father knows what he's doing," my mother insisted. Seeing the bus arrive, the door open, I felt like bait about to be consumed. Up and down the hilly dirt roads the bus would rattle and shake its way to the school.

The building had a gravel yard surrounded by a high wire fence. At recess and at lunch I would stand in the building's shadow, hoping to avoid the blows of the farmers' and store-keepers' children. By the time they found out that I was also a Jew, it was too late; by then I was Benjamin Bear, only eleven years old but already over five feet tall and heavily built. And I was already one of them. Instead of studying like a good professor's son I spent all my time in the fields or the barns; instead of following my father's refined and intellectual footsteps I was the star defenceman on the public school hockey team, my eyebrows quickly decorated with scars, one front tooth chipped, worse to come.

"You hated that school to begin with," my father told me once. As if I didn't know. It was an October Saturday and we were driving by the school on the way to get winter grain for the cattle. I had been looking not at the school but at the maple bush beyond, where I had wanted to go hunting that day with the Spencer boys. My father was wearing workboots that worked only on weekends, jeans showily stained with grease from the tractor. When I went to town with my father, when I worked with him in the barn or helped him lift heavy sacks of molasses-soaked grain into the truck, my job was to protect him from straining himself or going beyond his limits; as though my father was one of those animals I was always finding in the fields, a dark-eyed, narrow-faced animal with delicate bones and teeth too fragile to bite its enemies, a runt fox, a sharp little creature who looked great on the run, but weak and timorous in repose.

"It was a question of principle. I could have driven you to Kingston every day but I wanted you to go to the same school as your neighbours. Otherwise you would never have made friends."

We were on the highway. My father was driving too slowly, and the fence posts were dragging by one at a time. In the pit of my stomach I had that uncomfortable feeling that always warned me bad news was coming. Like the day, for example, when we were driving to town and my father announced I would be spending the summer at a French music camp.

"A French music camp?"

"It's time you started on a second language. A Canadian who speaks only one language is only half a person. And I want you to learn a musical instrument too. My father had a violin. He gave it to me when I was your age. Now I'm going to give it to you. Would you like that?"

"What do I need to learn French for? No one around here talks French."

"They used to," my father said. "The man who first cleared our farm was a Frenchman. He sent his son to the First World War and his son lost his leg. Then he came back here and built the big barn."

My father had lit up one of the small cigars he smoked on the way to town. Because the son of a Frenchman had got his leg shot off, I, Benjamin Winters, had to learn to speak French. It was a familiar kind of equation. For example: because the Germans had baked six million Jews, I, Benjamin Winters, was one day going to have to have a bar mitzvah in a Kingston synagogue.

My stomach began to knot. "Your mother and I have been talking about your education." As if, in the old farmhouse my father had bought and renovated, there was such a thing as a word that could be spoken in privacy. "As you know, you're not going to want to live here all your life. A few years from now and you'll be dying to get away."

I was slouched into the corner of the seat. The sky was cloudy, a skeiny grey cloud that kept the air warm but was too thin to rain. Later on the cloud would start to pull apart, by the end of the day the sky would be yellow and soft around the edges, and the moist air over the lake sweet and decaying. That was where I wanted to be—on the lake. In fact I hadn't wanted to go to town at all; school had started only four weeks ago and I had been counting on spending the day outside, away from buildings and the demanding voices of adults. I opened the truck window. The air rushed in, caught the tip of my father's cigar; when he turned to speak sparks exploded in his face.

*5. Meanwhile, My Father: Part II, or,*
*Group Portrait with Voice*


"David and Benjamin Winters," Helen once said to me. "When I first heard your names I thought you must be some kind of father and son team." Some kind of biblical father and son team, I thought she meant. My mother also made biblical references to my father: the old King David who liked to keep his body warm with young girls. It was true, in fact, that in my father's house the telephone might at any time ring with a woman's voice on the other end. At least one such voice was recorded on his answering machine. This was during one of the marital reconciliations, just after my father had sent Ruth and me identical letters on his PROFESSOR DAVID WINTERS stationery announcing that we had joint parents again. The four of us had come in from a restaurant, an excursion arranged to celebrate, and my mother had switched on the machine.

"It's me," the voice emerged. This disembodied voice, a surprise visitor in our kitchen, was larger than any person could have been. We stood there and listened. The surreal clinking of glasses, a blurring of sound—we could all imagine the slightly drunk sad woman at the other end—a drunk sad woman not so different from my mother on too many occasions—"Where have you been? You promised to come over this afternoon." More sounds, as though the traffic were driving through her open window, a rasping indecisive cough followed by "Christ, David, you're such an asshole"—and then the dialtone.

After I had been playing hockey for a few years I thought I knew the kind of man my father was, a small man with a lot to prove. But when I was younger I had actually wished we could be a team. That was our first year in the country; when I saw the other farmers driving about with signs on their trucks like *Richardson & Sons* I hoped my father might one day put *Winters & Son* on the old truck he had bought to play farmer with.

David: when I was younger everyone called him Dr. Winters or Professor Winters or just plain Professor. My mother was the exception. Nor did she go for terms of endearment. "Honey, sweetie, dear," she would say derisively, "doesn't it just make you sick to see women on their knees? Honey, sweetie, dear— no one with any self-respect could let that garbage slide over her tongue."

"It must be strange to have such an important father," Helen said to me another time. She was ashamed of her own father. He lived in a sensible house in Port Hope, where he owned an insurance agency. They also had a cottage fifty miles north, a cottage that was, like their nineteenth-century home, perfectly maintained. He drank.

The night that unidentified woman's voice came to visit, we should have had our picture taken. My father, Professor Doctor David Winters, afraid to leave the room, leaned against the doorjamb with his eyes closed: the condemned man waiting to be shot. Ruth sat down on the bench of the built-in breakfast table. Like me she was biting the insides of her cheeks, the way we'd taught each other to keep from laughing during moments of matrimonial comedy. She was also hating my father: I could tell by the funny way the skin around her eyes had bunched and muscled, the same way it had the night she got drunk, told me everything she knew about what he was doing and called him "that cheap, cheap, cheap sleazoid."

My mother was the only one not frozen. On the contrary, she was all motion, almost dancing; as from the tape machine squawked that stranger's voice, as it surrounded itself with the noises of traffic, the blur of drunkenness, sorrow, as our kitchen suddenly became the stage and that voice presented its brief Act One of loneliness, my mother glided into action, head twitching and nodding with agreement, fingers snapping, under-the-breath comments we couldn't quite catch taunting my father.

When the machine clicked off, leaving us alone in our family kitchen, my mother spread her arms wide, stamped her feet into position the way she used to before singing all the tunes from *The Wizard of Oz*, then rolled her eyes up so high only tiny cusps of her pupils could be seen. Slowly, slowly, she turned from my father to Ruth and me. At that moment, suddenly feeling truly sorry for my father, I wished he could make a joke, break the spell, say whatever it took for the disaster to turn into something else. But he just waited, struck dumb by his misfortune, upstaged even at the moment of his own downfall as my mother, in her stagiest husky voice, announced: "My children, that's one *bad* witch."

*6. The Touch*

I left Levin's office without answering him and went to my car. When I looked back at the house I could see the windows shining at me like large blank mirrors. I turned on the motor. A few afternoons ago Timmy—my son and so far the only grandchild—had helped me take out the spark plugs, clean them with knives and steel wool. He had rubbed and scrubbed as though the world depended on it; and when he was allowed to twist them back into place his face had glowed with triumph. Timmy, it seemed, was always alight with triumph or disaster.

Once out of the driveway, I continued slowly along the road. Look, Mother—see your son on his way to hearth and home. But when the winding road leading to Heritage Acres funnelled into a larger road, when my mother, my brother-in-law, Norton Meredith, even my mother's nurse Julia could no longer see me, I—instead of turning towards the highway—took the other direction. Still I drove slowly, and even when I had parked once again, this time in front of the apartment building, I wondered if I had remembered correctly, in daylight, the drive I had previously made in the dark. Then I was at the door. The pain in my stomach was gone but my heart was pounding the way it used to before a big game or an exam. But not before something like this because—at least in certain essential details—this was new. The key was under the doormat. I let myself in, hung my jacket carefully in the closet. The living-room drapes were drawn, the apartment was filled with a cool gauzy light. There was a stereo in an old-fashioned wooden cabinet. I put on the record that had been the excuse for the first meeting here, *Ella Fitzgerald Live*, and lay down on my back on the couch.

After one of my visits to Heritage Acres Julia had come up to me and said she knew I wouldn't remember, but she had met me once before, when her name was Julia Collins. That was after a hockey game when I played for the Queen's University team and her boyfriend had taken her to what—as it turned out—was the last game of the playoffs.

"I'm married now," was all I could say.

"Of course you're married. I know all about you, remember? Your mother talks about you every day."

I was frightened by what I was doing. Ella Fitzgerald's voice drifted through the living room like smoke over a bar. Like Julia's smoky grey eyes that always looked at me without blinking. In the lounge, one rainy June Sunday while I was waiting for my mother to come down, she'd put on a Miles Davis record. I'd gone to see what it was. "You like jazz?"

"Some."

"That's interesting."

"Interesting?"

"A hockey player liking jazz."

"I retired."

"That's right. You told me. Now you're married."

All the time her eyes were on me, sweet and sour. Julia was, I was thinking, one of those women who seemed to invite without wanting to, who disliked men who refused to understand that the invitation wasn't for them. But I couldn't help noticing her smooth velvety skin. And, of course, the obligatory large breasts: Levin, hiring, stayed true to his college-boy fixation. And then, without warning, everything changed. I was suddenly aware of my breathing, of hers, of the way our bodies were adjusting to each other across the table.

I had never been unfaithful to Helen before, never wanted to. A matter of principle, I suppose: the principle being that I didn't want to be like my father. At first I even promised myself that I would love Helen better than he had loved Melanie. But then—when I first loved Helen—I hadn't asked myself how Helen might love me. How her love for me might gradually flow into Timmy, into the farm, into the beans and tomatoes and radishes and berries which spent so much more time in her hands than did the flesh of her husband. I heard a noise in the hall. I sat up. I remembered Levin telling me about a patient who'd tried to have an affair, but found himself impotently thinking about his children at what was supposed to be the big moment.

What might be the big moment with Julia? The first time—the last time—the only time I'd been here, we hadn't touched. Julia's perfume had smelled of late-summer honey, a dark whirlpool out of season for a married man with a young child.

"I don't fall in love," Julia had told me as I was leaving. To reassure me, I suppose, but instead giving me the sudden unwanted image of her ex-husband standing at this same door, drinking in this same cool perfection, listening to his wife inform him that she was his no longer, never had been, belonged only to herself, a loan from the library of love that must now be returned.

Now I was back. I wanted to be here; even reading in the newspaper that one in twelve North Americans was addicted to sex had failed to discourage me. Standing in the middle of the living room, trembling with—fear? desire?—I had no doubt that having sex with Julia would break apart my life. Such as it was. The shell I had so carefully constructed—like a spider trying to make a brick house out of spit—since I left medical school ten years ago.

But thanks to Helen my life had mended. We had married. Helen had given us Timmy. Or Timmy had appeared. Even in the apartment of another woman, *especially* in this apartment, I found myself remembering the actual birth, Helen's superhuman effort to expel Timmy into my hands. Her serene smile afterwards, having endured the unendurable. This is the kind of bond that can never break, I said to myself that morning. Nor did it—though it could strangle, go slack, disappear for months on end.

Before being the perfect mother, Helen had been the perfect wife-designate, a dark-haired brainchild writing her thesis under my father's supervision. So brilliant, so long of dark shining hair, that my father, Professor Doctor David Winters, had hired her as a summer research assistant. That was during one of the marital "intermissions", when my mother was living in a Kingston apartment and taking primal scream therapy. To ease the separation, I had been divided between my parents: weekdays in the city to keep my mother company during her night-time relapses, weekends on the farm to help my father with the crops. I was still in medical school then, getting ready to specialize in psychiatry. When I arrived at the farmhouse to discover Helen installed, I decided that my father was overdue for his own visit to Uncle Sigmund. Everything Helen said, I contradicted. She argued back. I was shouting when I realized my hand was wrapped around a bottle of wine, not the first. I offered a midnight canoe ride. Helen refused. My father insisted. We went down to the lake in grumpy silence. Ten feet out from shore, as I was swinging the paddle towards the piercing cry of a loon, the canoe did a quick shake and sent us into the water.

In those early days her voice had sounded different to me. Because, no doubt, there were certain things she had not yet said. "You're *covered* with hair," she exclaimed that first night. "I bet all the girls want you to take them to bed and keep them warm for ever."

"Just you."

"I didn't say anything about us." But soon we were spending almost every night together. When one morning it came to me, not exactly a surprise, that I didn't want to finish medical school, didn't want to be a doctor, didn't want to be someone who drove a fancy car, sent his children to private school, got messages from his mistress on the answering machine—when that morning I couldn't get up to do what I was supposed to do, Helen brought me coffee and looked out the window.

In those early days, when her voice sounded all sweetness, looking silently out the window was the height of eloquence. This was in Kingston: a big sun-flooded bay window. Helen was mysterious, self-contained, serene: watching how easily she accepted my decision made it easy for me. The next week I moved back to the farm, where, having obtained a "leave of absence" from the university, I started building an addition to the house. For therapy, my father told me; for the smell and feel of the wood, I told myself; for Helen and Timmy, it turned out.

Now Timmy was happy, living in his own golden bubble. But somehow I had fallen out. And now, it seemed, unable to control myself, I was about to start doing to Timmy what my own father had done to me. "You don't need to tell me," Julia had said. "Be there or not."

I called Helen at the farm to tell her I was going to have dinner in town. "Love you," she said, hanging up. Her voice was automatic and filled mostly with sympathy—as though she knew I was in a difficult position I might not be able to handle. It sent me to the front hall, where I stood looking at my coat as if it were a dog barking to go home.

I could hear the refrigerator motor, the elevator doors opening and closing. I was going to do this, do it once, and then it would be over.

"Bennie and Hennie," my mother called us. "I know everything about her," she had also said. But she didn't, nor did she like Helen any more than she would have liked anyone else. Thinking of my mother's dislike for Helen, the errant son finally became the loyal husband. Once more I went to the front hall. The door opened. Julia was standing in front of me, her face open and smiling. The only space left between us was filled up by our clothes.

"I don't do this," she said later.

"Neither do I." It was almost midnight. I was already wondering what I would say to Helen. I was remembering that I had promised myself once would be enough. I was remembering that Julia had told me she didn't fall in love. I was wondering if Levin and my sister had ever turned their bodies inside out. *You got the itch?*

**II**

## 1. Two Interviews with Christopher Lewis

Christopher Lewis leaned towards the coffee on the tray Rabbi Goldman's wife had placed on his desk. "Dresden china," she said, as the black muddy pool quivered. "My parents came from Dresden, they were shot in the street." Christopher hesitated, the coffee halfway to his mouth. "Although I took no pleasure in seeing that city laid flat."

Rabbi Goldman smiled. He had generous lips surrounded by a neatly trimmed beard. "A question of divine retribution."

"But it gave *me* no pleasure," Mrs. Goldman insisted. Then she turned to Christopher. "What about you?"

Christopher, his tongue surrounded by the thick and bitter coffee, pointed helplessly to his mouth.

"You were in a camp," Mrs. Goldman said, "with this man who is coming?"

"Jakob Bronski," said the rabbi. "Jakob Bronski is the man who saved Mr. Lewis's life at Drancy. And now that Bronski is able to leave Moscow, Mr. Lewis is going to return the favour." The rabbi smiled again. He was an American but like Christopher he had been in Paris so long that he seemed to belong nowhere else than in Paris's perpetual nation of exiles.

"You mean," said Mrs. Goldman, "this is an act of attrition?"

"Contrition," the rabbi corrected.

"He's paying," Mrs. Goldman said, "is what I understand. He's ready to pay for his past and give this Jew a home."

"I'm only taking him there."

Rabbi Goldman looked sadly at Christopher and raised his eyebrows. Christopher knew what the rabbi meant. He meant that not only might Jakob Bronski need a home, but so might Christopher Lewis. This the rabbi had already explained at great length, on a previous visit. The kind of home Christopher Lewis needed, according to Rabbi Goldman, was a spiritual home. To prove this the rabbi had pulled out one of Christopher's own books, a historical mystery novel in which the final clue was found in the diary of a lunatic.

"The meaning of God is what you were writing about," the rabbi had suggested. "Because God is the mystery that drives us mad."

Now the rabbi set down his own coffee cup, poked absently at the grounds, looked at some papers on his desk. "According to information from our connections, Jakob Bronski should be here within a week. He is said to be old, but not crippled or senile. I quote to you from the document—'this man has not been an important actor on the stage of history, but considering what he has survived, it is a miracle that he is alive. He is a Jew who has transcended the status of victim to become a beacon of hope, a moral exemplar'—in any case, Mr. Lewis, you can see how enthusiastic our own people are about the release of Jakob Bronski. I wish you weren't taking him away from us so quickly but—"

"He means I'm curious," the rabbi's wife interrupted. "You wouldn't have seen my byline, but I write myself, just a reporter for the Jewish press in Philadelphia. With your permission I was hoping for—and with that of Mr. Bronski, of course—some sort of interview to commemorate his freedom." She paused. "In case you *have* seen it, I write under the name of Leah Goldman."

"To hear her speak you would think she was born in America. But believe me, it wasn't always like that. And writing! For you it is just putting pen to paper but for my wife it was sweating for years over dictionaries, grammar books, and all the classics, too, Jewish and goy. In this very apartment she read me *Julius Caesar*. It was like being in school again."

"Just a short interview with him and a picture. You wouldn't be aware, Mr. Lewis, but Jakob Bronski could be an important symbol to us Jews. A man like that gaining freedom after everything he has experienced. Some might call it a parable of faith, if you'll excuse me."

"My wife knows our faith means nothing to you, Mr. Lewis. But perhaps because you witnessed the camps—"

"Only one."

"I want to interview you as well," Leah Goldman offered. "A few questions to put the whole situation in perspective."

The rabbi suddenly stood up, pressed Christopher's hand with his own soft white palm, began to direct him to the door. "They sent pictures, too. I took them to be enlarged and I'm hoping to have them back today. When they're ready I'll send them to you." In the hall he squeezed Christopher's shoulder. "*Mazel tov*."

"Thank you," Christopher said.

The Goldman apartment was at the edge of the old Jewish clothing district. After he left, Christopher had been standing on the sidewalk outside, enjoying his own small taste of freedom while watching—across the street—a man in a Sikh turban painting out the sign from an old kosher butcher, when a window opened above and Leah Goldman dropped down a small packet of newspapers. This packet Christopher had transported to the Métro, held in his lap while being carried across Paris towards his own place, which was in an equally unfashionable spot on the Left Bank, shoved under his arm while he did his shopping and returned to his apartment. Then he had piled the newspapers on the kitchen counter and used them as a cutting board while he sliced tomatoes for a sandwich.

After the sandwich he slept, woke up, went out for dinner, took a bath at midnight and sat down at his desk to work on the movie script he had been avoiding. Now it was morning again.

He leaned over, turned off the typewriter. "Why do you write?" a reporter had once asked him and he had answered: "To drown out the noise of my typewriter motor." He extended his arms straight out, scarecrow style, opened his palms to the walls, rotated slowly. On another occasion he had described himself as a short man, comfortably wide due to long hours spent sitting at table during mealtimes. That had been quite a few years ago, in the era when he had been able to say, almost truthfully, that he was his own best critic. Since then the competition had intensified. Pinned above his desk, little reminders to keep the adrenalin going, were two notices of his latest book. One from the London *Sunday Times* was very short. His novel, the third and last of a series about Henry II, was reviewed along with two other historical novels by writers who, the reviewer had pointed out, "were new and worthy pretenders to the throne which, sadly, it now becomes clear Christopher Lewis was never able to occupy." The other review was much larger. Titled "Christopher Lewis At 58", it was centred on a recent picture—a good one, Christopher had thought, before he saw it in context. The photograph had been taken outside: his face was round and tanned, his eyes crinkled because of the sun, the remains of his straight silvery hair made him look almost distinguished. "Not A Bang But A Whimper" the cut-line read.

He opened the windows. A choir of sirens filled the room. Somewhere a politician was already on the move, surrounded by a shell of police cars and motorcycles. It was eight in the morning and the clear sky over Paris was stained at the horizon by a narrow edge of pollution. By noon the general din of diesel engines, traffic jams, ambulances practising steeplechase, would make it impossible for any single noise to be noticed. And by noon the polluted edge of the sky would be invisible, not because it had disappeared but because it would have risen to cover the whole city in a reddish-gold haze. For the moment, everything was contained. Noise, toxic chemicals, colliding masses of population were suspended in perfect balance.

Temporary balance. The temporary balance that was perfection. Or vice versa.

Christopher put his hands on his hips, tried to make his torso go in circles while his legs stayed unmoving. Arthritic? Somewhat. Overweight? Undeniably. On the edges of the desk and on the floor were the pages he had written that night. Stacked together, they made a pile, but just looking at them gave Christopher an unwelcome stab.

Also on the floor, spread face-down, was *Ape Man*. This was the novel from which the movie was being made, for which he was supposed to be writing the script. The movie deal had given his agent, Lucy Chadwick, the ammunition to get it back into print, so aside from remainders of his latest and less popular efforts, *Ape Man* was the opus by which he was currently represented in bookstores.

It had been published twenty years ago. The blow-by-blow story of a beautiful young American art student and an eminent historian, both of whom took up anthropology as a hobby. And, in the novel, these two lost souls—alienated North Americans wandering the African desert—found both a valuable historic skeleton and a love sufficiently primitive that it remade their lives. The teller of the novel, a young and yearning museum worker, was of course a thinly disguised version of Christopher himself—who after finishing school had been given a job in a museum by a friend of his mother's. And the lovestruck couple had been David and Melanie—to whom the book was dedicated. "Forgive the lack of sex scenes," Christopher had joked when he presented them with their copy. "You both wore so little on the expedition that there was nothing left for me to invent." And so they had forgiven him: the sex scenes which in fact the novel did not lack, the dialogue stolen from dinners around the campfire, even the hilarious portrayal of David's wealthy fiancée arriving in a helicopter. Emerging from a cloud of dust like a malevolent genie, she had rushed up to David Winters and screamed: "I know what you're doing! You asshole! You're humiliating me!" Then she had turned around, marched back to the helicopter, flown away into the infinite blue sky over Kenya.

Christopher stood at the sink. He closed his eyes. A wave of fatigue rolled through him. He imagined himself lying on his back in the sand. He had done that late one afternoon, fitting the sand around hip and shoulders, a warm cocoon of sleep. When he woke up it was twilight. Melanie was sitting cross-legged in front of him, unaware he was watching, all attention on a monkey's skull she was picking clean with a knife. She was a vision: glowing long hair, tanned skin, skimpy halter falling forward to reveal lush white breasts capped with pink untouchable petals. He had closed his eyes, then coughed so she would know he had woken.

Christopher sat down. An hour ago he had been feeling perfect, vital, indomitable. Now he ached. Sometimes the ache he felt for women was, though sharp and even unpleasant, an ache that could be—might be—satisfied. But this feeling he had for Melanie was a different kind of feeling; it was the desire for the past, the yearning to be drunk on a vintage no longer for sale. "I lusted after your wife when she was young," he imagined himself telling David. In the strange ritual orgy which had provided the climax to the book she had given herself first to the curator, then to her husband-to-be. Except that, in real life, David had gone back to the rich fiancée in the helicopter. He hadn't been ready for Melanie, yet. And also, in real life, there had been no orgy. Not even an orgy with a description of the sex act omitted. "He had been," Christopher had written of the young curator, "transported beyond himself. Wrapped in the arms of his goddess, feasting on her, he felt his mind break open under the pressure of the desert night. When it was over he knew that he had not possessed her, but that he himself had been possessed, taken over, run through by a psychic tornado of confused passion that had been released by their summer of digging into the earth's crust. Now the passion was past. He was as much apart from her as he had been before. She was, if anything, even more unattainable, more remote."

That book, romance-inspired bullshit included, had taken him almost five years to write. Days at the museum, sorting and classifying the bones found on the expedition, nights at his tiny Regent's Park flat, writing by hand because the landlady, who lived below, had told him that "tenants must choose between the evils of female visitors and noise." Then, too, it had been the bath at midnight followed by six hours unmoving at the desk. At dawn he would hurry out to Regent's Park and run through the mist and hills as though he were back in Africa, back at the beginning of the world, back at the dizzy crescendo of life when the planet was exploding with energy, when mind and heart beat to the same wild drum. Or at least, Christopher said to himself, standing in front of his bathroom mirror and carefully shaving away wide stripes of white lather, the drum had seemed to be wild and life had seemed to be a dizzy crescendo of open possibility.

"Feel my heart." He had taken her literally, the way he knew she wanted to be taken, the way everything was taken at Drancy. Her heart had struggled against the pressure of his hand. "Christopher, I'm going to die," she had announced. Then giggled at the melodramatic tone of her voice.

That was February 14, 1944. Valentine's night. By then everyone knew that the net was tightening around the Third Reich, and that in only a few months the war would be over. Drancy was at times half empty and forgetful of its mission. There were even rumours that the Paris police were refusing to pick up Jews as instructed. Until a new list was posted, a new death train scheduled to be filled. Tomorrow it was to be their turn on the train. Heavy rains sweeping the concrete walls. Night time. Bones shaking with cold. He must have imagined the whiteness of her skin. But the heart: he could still feel the blood rising like a tide into his palm.

When his head was shaved Christopher was first of all surprised at how cold it suddenly was, how much more sensitive was his naked scalp than any other part of his body. He had reached up to touch it. A sandpapery feel, patches of bristle, bony knobs and smooth expanses. Kneeling like dogs, head to head, they had rubbed their skulls together. Then side by side, his hand on her heart. The rain in bursts against the wall. She had undone his pants. Run her hands the length of his body. "So you don't die untouched," she had said. He had been fifteen years old then, Melanie eleven, but both so thin and stunted by lack of food that they still looked like children. The cells Melanie had touched had long ago been recycled and replaced. But the nerves remembered the tug of her fingers. The surprising collisions of bone.

"Feel my heart," she had commanded.

Eventually Jakob Bronski, their long-time protector, found them in their corner. He was as thin as old sticks. He walked always bent forward, peering through the glasses someone had given him to replace his own. He explained to them that once he had been father to an infant daughter. That he had abandoned her and they had become his children in her place. That after death they would all be reunited in heaven under God's eyes, or that perhaps there was no such thing as either God or compassion. He asked their opinion. They talked all night about God or His absence. As though God really existed or really did not. As though what they decided truly mattered.

"Love, for example," Jakob Bronski had said. "Here I have found the love of many people, given love to many people. If God is love, then God definitely exists, don't you agree?"

"But what if God is compassion?" Melanie had asked. They were in a corner, the three of them. Melanie and Christopher under the same blanket. Melanie holding tight to Christopher's hand. A silence; an ominous gap finally filled by new bursts of wind and rain. A tide of cold making their jaws clatter all at once like a symphony of bones. Melanie, throwing her arms open wide. "I am dying, my loves, dying." Jakob was the first to laugh.

In the morning they were told the engines had broken down. The rains grew stronger, heavier, pounded the yards of Drancy into icy swamps of misery. By the time the trains could be repaired weeks had passed. New lists had been made up.

Christopher and Melanie were spared; it was Jakob who was taken.

At the end of the summer Paris was liberated and Christopher and Melanie found themselves in the hands of the Americans. Melanie, whose parents were never located, was sent home to live with relatives in America. Christopher, whose journalist father had brought his family to France just before the invasion, wrote a letter to his mother at her old address: it was forwarded to her new place—her own mother's apartment in London— and a few weeks later Christopher was reunited with them.

"I always thought something tragic must have happened to you during the war," his agent once said to him. "Something that fixed you on Paris and made you return—despite what happened to you there."

Lucy Chadwick had emigrated from New York to London a few years after the war to start a literary agency. All of this while packaged as a brassy dyed blonde, a 1950s-style broad who still used cigarette holders.

"Of course you don't like to talk about it. I remember reading your first novel, *Past Perfect*, such a happy book about your childhood; this man must be miserable, I said to myself. Still, what a glorious beginning you had. But you must have been tempted to write about the camp."

"Everyone else did it better."

"You mean you couldn't, because you weren't a Jew. But then, since you're not, you could write about Jews. Have you ever considered that?"

"Write about Jews?"

"Yes, write about Jews. You write about British kings, Greek sailors, Roman legislators, homosexual army officers, women in love with money. Why not Jews? If your time at the camp meant so much to you, you must have something to say about it. Why don't you try?"

This conversation had been occasioned by a liquid-soaked dinner to celebrate the signing of the movie contract for *Ape Man*.

41

"Don't give me the deep freeze, Christopher. We've known each other for thirty years. I'm the faithful admirer, aren't I? I'm the one who sought you out, courted you, signed you, siphoned money to you, offered everything but my body—no one wanted it anyway—to get the best for your books. And the whole time watched you limping your way through life, the walking wounded. Why don't you get it out of your system? You know what I wonder about you, Christopher? About all men? Do you ever come clean with yourselves? Do you ever really know what you feel? Why do women do all the feeling in this world while men just look at them, the way you're looking at me? Is there something so holy that happened to you in that camp that you can't tell a living soul? Are you the only person who ever watched another person die? It must have been strange, Christopher, you—a Christian even if you didn't go to church—watching all those Jews getting sent off to the ovens. I mean, Christopher, what did it *feel* like to watch them go?"

I could have gone too, he might have said to her. Or even told her about the time his name *was* put on the list. But he knew that wasn't what Lucy really wanted. Although he had an answer for himself. To himself he had said that while at Drancy he had felt like his father the journalist, like the writer he eventually became, a reporter plunged into the action, subject to the dangers of the action, but not truly part of it. Which meant, to be exact, that while the action was happening all around him, the centre of the action was not his own centre, which was a place walled off, defended, observing. At least during the first few months at the camp he had considered himself apart from those Jews. Those pariahs. Those self-selected victims. Looking at the men's unshaven and fearful faces, the women's filthy clothes and mouths gaping in permanent anguish, seeing the Jew children wandering desperately in their parents' lee—or worse, seeking missing parents—he felt above, beyond, immune. Until the time a guard's boot buried itself in his ribs and he was lying on the ground without even the breath to shout his pain; and then the boot had swung again, breaking his front teeth and mixing their chips with his blood so that when finally he could take a breath it was only to spit free—only then had he for the first time heard, really heard, the voice of the Jews. And that voice was an ear-splitting scream of rage, Melanie's, as she launched herself at the guard. There was the seed of what Lucy wanted. What Lucy wanted was his mind's-eye portrait of the eternal Jew: a dying girl crying with rage while a great clawed bird flew from her open mouth to shit its vengeance on the world.

He washed the lather from his face, stripped, took a shower. Then he put on his underpants and lay face-down on his bed.

He was a big man; his wintry skin covered a broad back, a spare tire that bulged at the waist, thick arms and legs. Hard to believe that he had almost starved at Drancy. That as a young man he had been photographed in Africa, bronzed, lean, naked except for a pair of baggy army shorts.

He was dreaming that a special-delivery letter was winging its way towards him, one beginning *Dear Mr. Lewis, the Chancellor has asked me to inform you that your salary has been raised to sixteen million francs a month commencing...*, when he became aware of the slow chugging shuffle with which his concierge mounted the stairs. There were four flights; her heavy breathing began at the very first step. "Each person must do their duty," she had finally said to him—not without making it clear that she considered him hopeless in this area—when he had offered to pick up his own mail. None the less, she now ascended only for impressive-looking packages, packages that would make a satisfying *clump*, as this one did as she gave it the martyr's toss from the top landing to his door. When she had started down again Christopher opened the door. The *clump* had been made by a wad composed of several letters and a large brown envelope. One of the letters was a telephone bill, two were from the Boston ladies' college on whose behalf he had dreamed so sweetly.

The brown envelope had a Paris postmark. Christopher slit it open. Sandwiched between cardboard squares were the photographs, enlarged and glossy, promised by Rabbi Goldman. It was easy to see that these photographs had begun their lives as snapshots—enlargement had preserved the grains and wrinkles; and so many years separated them that their subject might have been three different men.

The first showed Jakob Bronski in Paris. It was dated 1937 and displayed a thin, bespectacled Bronski, wearing a dark suit and tie. The picture had been taken out of doors. Bronski was smiling, and behind him was the shimmering light reflected from the pond of—according to the inscription on the back of the photograph—the Luxembourg Gardens. In the second photograph, the one that had been used in all the British newspapers in the 1950s, Bronski was wearing baggy slacks and an open-necked white shirt. This too had been taken outside; in the background was the mental hospital at which he had been first inmate, then staff member. By now the smooth regular features of the young man had grown harsher; the body had changed from one belonging to a carefree intellectual to the thicker, irregular body of a man who had spent a certain number of years wielding shovels, axes, sledgehammers; the black hair combed low and parted to the side had receded and was austerely brushed straight back.

In the third photograph, taken only a few months ago, time was the villain. The hope of the young man, the haggard insistence of the middle-aged one, had been replaced by fatigue. Face and shoulders had grown heavier yet; one eye looked directly at the camera while the other was half closed in resignation.

## 2. One Interview with Jakob Bronski

It was this simple: the airplane, which for hours had been suspended between Moscow and Paris, suddenly began to lose speed.

The man in the third photograph looked at his hands.

A bumpy landing, the doors opening, a quick trip in the shuttlebus during which he pushed out his chest to feel the weight of the magic papers folded in the inside pockets of his jacket. For a moment the sun was in his eyes; he walked, he blinked, then Rabbi Goldman—carrying a sign—was standing in front of him. Smiling, speaking, grasping his shoulders and kissing his cheeks. Behind the rabbi was his wife, a camera slung over her shoulder.

They dropped his suitcase off at the hotel, then brought him back to their apartment for breakfast. Jakob Bronski found himself staring at his shoes. They were large and bulged irregularly. In Moscow, only two nights ago, he had polished them. In the dim lamplight the shoes had glowed with promise, a rich unheard-of lustre that had arrested Bronski in the midst of his preparations. Shoe polish! What a miracle! Maybe he should have used it before. Now the black polish was already splotchy and mottled; on the fancy rug his shoes looked out of place, half-covered refugees that should have been buried long ago.

"It must be very moving for you to be back in Paris," Leah Goldman proposed. She had a square, almost mannish face, but there was something peculiar and delicate about the curve of her chin, something imperfect that kept making him want to reach out and reshape it. Or perhaps it was her mouth that he wanted to reshape—seal to be exact—with its endless probings and proddings.

On one knee she had placed a notepad. Already pages had been covered with shorthand jottings. Beside her, on the sofa, was the camera—still waiting in its leather case.

The rabbi was sitting at the dining-room table, pretending to read the newspaper he had inserted into the remains of breakfast, but every few seconds giving Jakob an apologetic look.

"Or perhaps you are too exhausted to truly enjoy your triumph?"

"I'm tired," Jakob said.

"Tired but happy?"

"Happy but tired."

The rabbi's wife smiled. I could tell you about trying to make people smile, Jakob thought. Her teeth were white, well cared for, just irregular enough to seem real.

"You don't look happy to me," Leah Goldman said. "I don't think of you as a happy man. Do you think of yourself as happy?"

Jakob imagined the article this woman would write. "No, of course not. But could I be permitted to be happy sometimes even if not"—he struggled for the word—"in general?"

"I have always thought of us Jews as a happy people. Inside, I mean. A people capable of great joy. Not at the suffering of others. For example, yesterday I was telling your friend that the bombing of Dresden gave me no pleasure. Even the news that Hitler was dead. Why should others suffer? I have always asked myself. Believe me, despite everything, cruelty is no thrill to someone like myself. Most important is the statement of life you make from inside yourself. Don't you think? Of course, with the tragedies, our lives have not been normal. But—"

She shifted her pad to the other knee, all the while looking up at Jakob, her mouth slightly open. As if by appearing on the edge of speech herself she could get him to come out with what she wanted. Jakob found his own mouth starting to twitch in response. It was true, in fact, that Paris was overwhelming him. Even from this apartment he felt bombarded by sounds, smells, glimpses down streets he hadn't seen for over forty years.

"Have you thought about the political stance you're going to take here? After almost fifty years of suffering for being a Jew, how do you react to criticism of what the Jews are doing to the Palestinians in Israel? My husband told me that when your exit visa was finally granted by Moscow, you turned down a professorship at the Hebrew University in Jerusalem."

In the taxi, while travelling from airport to hotel to the apartment, she had managed to verify her typed chronology of his life: Warsaw, Paris, Drancy, the labour camps, the years of semi-exile in the north, the mental hospital, the final decade in Moscow — each place with its dates underlined, its address where possible, its iniquities and publications.

"You said you were tired."

"I am."

"Is it difficult for you speaking English?"

"I was an interpreter for many years. As you know."

"And you also did translations?"

Bronski nodded. Through the window the sun was shining directly into his face. A hot sleep-giving sun to which he wished he could give himself fully. He had almost moved to Israel for that alone—the dream of lying in the sun, being baked by the sun, having his memories finally unclench and flow away into the sun. His eyes were closed. He wasn't asleep but the idea that this woman might think him asleep was not unwelcome. Although sometime, another time which he couldn't possibly imagine but which might—like too many unimaginable things — find its moment of arrival, he would like to talk about the comfort of translating. Surrounded by dictionaries, lexicons, the thick meaningless government documents which he rendered from Russian into English or vice versa, he had felt the restfulness of total nihilism. Translating little chunks of the endless flow of propaganda, technical data, case histories, he pictured himself the linguistic mechanic of nothingness—straightening tortured syntax, clarifying what at base was totally blurry, spading, turning, nourishing gigantic piles of utter garble—under certain circumstances such mental oblivion could offer a vacation.

"All we need now is a picture and my husband can take you back to the hotel."

"Please, no picture, I feel very old today."

"You could just look up and smile."

"Please."

"The whole world is curious to see you."

"Not quite the whole world."

"You'd be surprised. I still remember first reading your poems. The shock—"

Jakob found himself blushing. As always, he had forgotten the poems. Why not? There hadn't been so many. A couple of dozen written when he was in the mental hospital. During the months they had been giving him drugs. The day the drugs stopped he had stopped writing, stopped having any desire to write, but meanwhile the poems were smuggled out and published in England. Fortunately Khrushchev had just died and the new leaders were anxious to be seen as eager to forgive. Although there was nothing to forgive, because the poems had been not political but love poems to another inmate—odes, rants, chants in memory of a woman who had ignited him, a giant-killing fireball of a woman who had set his guts on fire and then burned with him for a single month.

"We'd better take you to the hotel. I insist."

"You can just put me in a taxi."

Suddenly he could taste the hospital in his mouth. The sour grit of unwashed sheets clamped between his teeth. The smell of urine, rusting metal; the foul rising clouds from the boiling tubs of "stew" in the kitchen. And then one day, long after the poems, a letter had got through. It was from the little American girl he had known at Drancy, the girl for whom he would make up stories about imaginary animals in an imaginary zoo, a zoo not so different from their own. "From my hospital to yours," she had written, whether ironically or not, and explained that she had learned his name and address from a Jewish organization and was writing to know if he was the same Jakob Bronski she had known so many years ago in the camp outside Paris. Could it possibly be? Could she send him packages, clothes, books?

"Are you all right?"

The rabbi's wife was tugging at his arm. He tried to compose a sentence to reassure her, but found he couldn't remember her name.

She had his arm in her two hands, was gripping it tightly as though she were struggling to wake an oversize statue. He pulled himself upright, away from her. Strange the way he couldn't get his eyes off her chin—aggressive and straight when she was asking questions, strangely plump and curved in repose. "I'm afraid you have a political schizophrenia, comrade," he imagined himself saying. "Your face betrays political confusion, an uncertainty over sexual roles. Fortunately, Soviet medicine and good will on your part can combine to cure you. If you co-operate. If you can bear a small amount of pain. But women are able to bear pain, aren't they? Women are constructed for the absorption of pain." That was what they had told Anna.

The pain will pass
The cure will last
The body suffers for the sake of the mind
The mind softens and tears apart
Making way for purity
Of soul.

The rabbi, it emerged, had other obligations. Leah Goldman accompanied Bronski to the hotel and stood beside him at the desk as he asked for his key. Strange to be talking French again.

He had given up on French when the train to Auschwitz had crossed the French border. Just as he couldn't imagine ever speaking Russian again, now that he had left Moscow. But the French words had stayed locked away somewhere: when he opened his mouth they tumbled out, more or less of their own accord, not always in the right order.

"Shall I help you to your room?"

"No need."

"I insist."

When they were in the door she produced a bottle of cognac. "At least you'll take a drink with me? In honour of our friendship?"

"Try this," Jakob said. "I brought vodka." On the plane he had wanted a drink, and again at the airport. Now he unfastened one of the suitcases, plunged his fist into his clothes, found the bottle. While Leah Goldman held out the glasses, he poured carefully, then swallowed his in a gulp. Immediately the blood began to hammer at his ears, and the air in the room grew thick. He stumbled trying to reach the window.

"Let me."

As he fell she redirected him towards the bed. He was lying on his back, shoes and jacket off, pillows propped under his head while she smoothed a water-soaked cloth across his face.

The cool water dug into the corners of his eyes, ran in icy trickles down the sides of his face and his neck. "I feel so tired," he said. "My skin can't breathe." She unbuttoned his shirt, laid a wet towel on top of him.

"Do you want me to call a doctor?"

"No."

"Do you—"

"No." He watched her face. Saying no, he had learned, was a way to test people's characters. The skin always jumped a little off the face, like someone who had slipped in a patch of ice dancing crazily in the air for balance. Or, as he had described the test to Anna, someone who had slipped on dogshit—struggling to regain his balance and land on his feet, but wanting to arrive in a place different from the one he had left. In the case of this woman's face, this woman whose name he did not seem able to remember, the skin turned very briefly dark, contorted slightly as though it had been slapped, then settled back into the smooth, almost passively eager expression where it had started.

He closed his eyes. He could feel the microscopic shrinking of the damp towel as it yielded its wetness to the drier air above, his parched skin below. If only this woman would evaporate with the moisture, leave him lying here, drifting. Didn't she know what it had taken for him to arrive? The endless months of meetings, the hundreds of letters, the weeks of sleepless nights, the tearing up of roots, bonds, the final reading and destruction of his journals, his work, everything that might do damage.

He pushed himself up to demand she leave, then saw that she was crying.

"I didn't mean to hurt you," Jakob said.

"Mr. Bronski, please. It's only that I admire so much what you've done, I only wanted to spend more time with you — "

"More time."

"Excuse me. You must be exhausted."

Somehow the contents of his suitcase had spread themselves around the floor. He could see the rabbi's wife observing the mess. "It was because I packed the vodka under the shirts, and the shirts under the books," he said. "To keep them flat."

"At least let me put things back together for you." Without waiting she was on her knees, sorting and stacking. A strong woman: wide shoulders, a surprisingly narrow waist which then flared out again. When for a moment she was directly under the desk light he noticed the fine transparent hairs at the corners of her mouth. Anna had told him that hairs you could see through—in certain places—places on women—were always dyed. He tried to imagine this capable woman with the schizophrenic chin sitting in a room somewhere dyeing the hairs of her moustache. And what would the rabbi think of his wife submitting herself to such procedures?

She was holding the copies of his book of poems, Russian edition and English translation tied together along with a small

51

packet of reviews. "I thought you said you didn't remember these."

"Someone packed them for me."

"A wife?"

Bronski looked at this woman, this wife, this writer for the American Jewish press who filed time capsules from old wars, who dressed well, who took care of her body, who was curious. "Not a wife. A man."

She opened the English edition. "I could read to you from these. Would you like that?"

"No, please. I brought them only as a gift—"

"A souvenir?"

She was kneeling in front of him now and he was forced to consider her. Thick blonde hair heavily laced with grey. Precisely shaped eyebrows. Eyes set wide apart, curious—no, demanding. Perhaps it was still her mouth and chin that unsettled him. The lips somehow too full, too mobile, too ready to shape themselves into questions he didn't want to answer. For which he had no answer. A wide face, a handsome woman. After Anna died there had been a woman such as this—a wide-faced handsome woman who took care of him, consoled him. They had finally lived together for several years until he managed to get a job translating technical documents in Moscow.

"You want to go to sleep."

"I'm sorry."

"The vodka is very good."

Yes, it was good vodka—raw, powerful.

"Do you pray?"

He looked at Leah Goldman. *Do you pray*, she had asked him.

"I pray," she said. "I pray for the children who are starving or sick. I pray for the parents who have to watch their children suffer. I pray for the parents who live while their children have died. I pray for our God and I pray for the Messiah and I pray for the Jews who are fools enough, like me, to pray for God and the Messiah. I pray for the men around the world who are working when it is too hot or too cold or they are too drunk. I pray for all the women who even as I am praying are getting raped, punched out, stabbed. I pray for anyone who is crying and then I pray twice for anyone who would like to be crying but dares not. I pray for the Jews who are being oppressed, and I also pray for the Armenians, the Kurds, the native peoples of North and South America, the tribes of Africa who are starving and the tribes of Asia who are smuggling drugs. I pray for the guerrillas whose boots are filled with shit and I pray for the torturers who are chasing them. Not to bore you with the whole list, but every night I pray for hours. Lying on my back in my bed. Beside my husband. Sometimes, while he is wearing his *tefillin*, I pray to the television set. Last night I prayed to the sound of the toilet flushing. Last night my best prayers were for you. I prayed you would arrive. I prayed you would find happiness with your friends. I prayed they would make a nest for you, a place for your wounds to heal, a true home for your last years. I prayed you would find time for me. I prayed you would have the strength and courage to talk about your ordeal, the ordeals of others—"

Through his closed eyes he was riding her voice into the universe of darkness. A new cool sheet of wetness spread over him. His chest, his belly, his groin. Then suddenly the wetness was hot. He could feel her tongue licking, probing, caressing; feel the schizophrenic curve of her chin digging into him. The bed rocked as she climbed to straddle him. Didn't she know how the mind could be trained to leave the body? How, in more extreme situations, the soul learned to leave behind the mind? Meanwhile his scars, his shadow fingers, his broken knuckles were sliding up the silky insides of her thighs, sucking in the love juice; old nerves were leaping back to life, his hands were flexing and stretching, rubbing and annealing, opening and enclosing, making way, finally, for the inevitable.

She closed the curtains, leaving herself the fluorescent glow from the bathroom in which to work. First she pushed aside the towels. He was wearing suspenders, broad bands of black elastic stiffened with age. To get these off she had to lift his shoulders, one by one. Amazing how heavy they were; shifting his weight stretched the muscles of her own back, as though they too were elastic, waiting for their chance to snap. When the suspenders lay at his waist, spread out like the skeletons of butterfly wings, she reinforced herself with a sip of vodka. Impossible not to appreciate the precise state of his undress. Impossible not to admire the decaying beauty of the sleeping giant as he lay unmoving, immovable, a one-man mass grave who refused to be exhumed. To make this trip he had worn a shirt with gold studs at the wrists. She undid them carefully, placed them side by side on the bureau. Then, after much tugging and wriggling of the sleeping arms, she managed to get off his shirt. Now all that remained on his torso was a cotton undershirt, a singlet like the ones she had repacked into his suitcase. Above the scoop neck his chest was thick with flesh. She put her palm against it. The hair on his chest was amazingly thick and wiry—like a coat of steel wool. She slid her hand beneath the collar of his singlet so it was directly above the heart. Pound Thud Crash this heart was like a boiler furnace. Moving her hand again, she circled his chest. Fatty pillows over the pectorals, a waist like a tractor tire. One of his nipples was under her palm. She stroked it, felt it shrink and grow hard. She took her hand away, pulled a blanket over him. In her article she would talk about the beacon of conscience who had come to the West, this gifted poet whose silence had become his most eloquent protest. In the article Jakob Bronski would be portrayed as an intelligent, informed Jew who personified the inner stubbornness, the exquisite sensibility, the generosity of his race. She knelt beside his bed, putting her face close to his. His cheeks were slack, the stubble thick and spiky against her fingertips. She put her lips to his, let his sleeping breath fill her mouth. Then she moved back and took the camera from her purse. He was sleeping so deeply now, after everything he had been through, surely the flash would not disturb him.

For the first time in almost fifty years he was standing in a church. Fifty years, half a century—no insignificant chip off the whole slab. He moved forward until he was behind the last row of pews, then put out his hands to steady himself. From the front of the church he could hear the murmur of voices. Prayers? Confession? Tourists consulting their guides? Outside the air had been hot and steamy, a heavy animal panting; inside the coolness was filled with odours of wood and cement.

Fifty years, half a century: a hundred such lives would form a chain right back to the invention of God—temples, churches, synagogues, mosques—the rise and fall of everything. The inescapable register of pain he had inescapably become.

"*Ça te plaît?* Do you like it?" Delacroix's fresco, she meant. "Jakob's Struggle with the Angel." Not in the front of the church, but in its own little alcove off to the side, where he was standing now, looking at the large dark images he remembered as larger and darker yet. The woman who first brought him to it had hooked her arm into his and pressed against his side—for warmth, he had first thought, because it was winter and the combination of wind and rain had set them both shivering and given her the idea, she had said, of stopping in this church where she could introduce him to his namesake. In the now moving counterpoint of voices he could suddenly almost hear hers. A dry sardonic whispering voice that had sounded such a bittersweet refrain.

In the fresco Jakob was twisted towards heaven—perhaps because painters liked their subjects to twist in order to make huge muscles look even larger, better defined. Jakob, seeing the painting, had also felt himself twisting, rebelling inside. Straightening himself out, finally, only when he found himself riding that bittersweet refrain, climbing the rising tones of her voice, scaling the ladders of her ribs while she, with her nails, used his back to invent the map of her desire. And then, while he lay on his belly and she kissed the roads she had made in his flesh, Jakob had explained how as a child, hearing the story of his name, he had always thought the struggle would be of the mind and soul—not the body—and that the battle would be between temptation resisted and temptation triumphant.

Strange, Jakob thought, that even when he was a young man happily ascending the ladder of flesh, life had still been only ideas. Now that his eyes had finally grown accustomed to the darkness of the church, he saw the woman who had spoken to him. She was sitting on a chair. Doughy skin, greying hair that stood out from her head in a sparse cloud, heavily spotted hands wrapped around her thick cane. She sat as though she had been sitting all day, and she was watching the painted Jakob the way another person might sit in a park watching the comings and goings of the world.

He looked back to the fresco. When he had first seen it, Delacroix's Jakob had seemed impossibly old to his eyes. Where youth should have been were thick bones covered with slabs of meat, muscles, fur. Now that he could see his namesake from the other side of time, he could marvel at the power of those overstated muscles, the wholeness of those thick limbs, the supple grace of that heavily armoured body.

Jakob hadn't died. His angel hadn't died. Melanie and Christopher still lived. This very morning he had spoken to Melanie on the telephone. And even now Christopher was waiting to receive him, at an address Jakob had tucked into his pocket; an address to which he could go, if he pleased, or telephone, if he preferred. And tomorrow Christopher would be accompanying him on the airplane to begin his new life.

"*Ça va?*"

Jakob turned towards the old woman. She was looking at him—not exactly staring. Her hands were trembling on her cane. On an impulse he stepped towards her, covered her hands with his own.

Without moving, she looked at his missing fingers, his scarred and lumpy skin. "*Ça va?*" she repeated.

"*Oui, ça va,*" Jakob said. The woman's eyes had turned back to his face, opened wider. One was a dark blue jewel. The other had clouded over. Tears began to leak from the corners, zigzag slowly down the network of her cheeks. But beneath his, her hands had stilled.

Jakob knelt before her. She was staring at him now, transfixed. He wondered if she was terrified, if she was sitting without moving in the hope that he would somehow forget she was there and go away.

She gripped his wrist. *"Le bon dieu—"*

He waited but instead of continuing she only repeated, *"le bon dieu, le bon dieu, le bon dieu...."* Lifting her hands to his mouth Jakob kissed her fingers.

She let go. He stood. He bowed. He made his way slowly to the door. From the front of the church he could hear the voices more clearly now, two women talking to each other in a rapid Italian of which he understood nothing. He turned back to the old woman. She was lost in the painting again. How wonderful it would be, he suddenly thought, if fifty years could just drop away, if the nightmare could go back to being the unknown future, if he could be once again stepping out into the rain with his young woman friend—

The sun was in his eyes. On his back he could feel once more the map of desire. A whole network of long-forgotten streets shimmered before him. The drugs, he suddenly realized, the drugs at the mental hospital had drowned the memory, the map, the knowledge of the streets and where those streets could lead. He saw himself standing at the bottom of a stairway, looking up to the woman who had drawn the map. And then her face was obliterated by the sun, in its place a baby, a scream splitting apart the emptiness—

In front of him was a car. The doors were slamming, the passengers leapt and swarmed towards him. His breath caught and his hand jerked up to his pocket where he kept his passport. They were carrying guidebooks and cameras. They were laughing. They had no interest in him.

## 3. Christopher and Jakob

Bronski was waiting for him in the hotel lobby. Sitting awkwardly on a sofa, large head thrust forward, reading a newspaper, he didn't at first seem to notice Christopher's entrance. Then, just as Christopher was about to speak, Bronski pushed aside the newspaper, put his hands on either side of himself, shoved down on the cushions with such force that his huge body floated upward like a spacebound rocket. The Jakob Bronski Christopher had known at Drancy had been fine, almost elegant; this man was raw and unfinished, a huge rusting machine of a man whose outstretched hands finally landed like cast iron on Christopher's shoulders.

"Is it you?"

"Who else?"

*And if it isn't?* Christopher wondered. But he was leaning closer to Bronski, the startling topography of his face, the new landscape of flesh in which he finally recognized the eyes, eyes that had once followed him day and night. Long afterwards he had realized how strange it was that Bronski—who had spent his whole life moving from one provisional escape to the next—could have made him believe in the security of his own British childhood, made him believe that the war, the camp, the traffic in unspeakable events were only temporary interruptions.

"Dinner?"

"Please," Bronski said. At the camp inviting each other for dinner had been one of their ways of passing the time. Once a week Bronski would take Melanie and Christopher aside and announce to them that Adolf Hitler had personally selected a famous Paris restaurant for their evening dining pleasure. Ushering them to a corner, Jakob would seat them with great ceremony; then he would explain the whole menu to them, headwaiter-style, counselling certain courses because the ingredients were particularly fresh, warning them away from others because the chef of his imaginary restaurant was in fact a Polish émigré—a suspected Jew who put certain classic items on the menu in order to appear more French. "The white sauce," Bronski always reminded them—"these Jews have no *idea* how to make white sauce. In this man's hands white sauce is an insult to the Aryan race."

"Something with white sauce?" Christopher now proposed.

"To tell the truth I detest French food."

"Greek then."

When they got to the restaurant, a tourist trap where Christopher both knew the owner and had so far escaped food poisoning, they stood outside for a moment. The sidewalk tables were filled; men in their shirtsleeves, women in thin dresses. All drinking red wine, talking English, German, Dutch, soaking themselves in the oversweet ambience of Left Bank Paris.

There was one free table; there they could have watched the play of the searchlights of the *bateaux-mouches* and inhaled the ripe odours of the Seine. But Jakob, leading the way, went inside, installed himself at a big empty table with his back to one of the smoke-stained walls.

Despite the muggy heat, Bronski had insisted on wearing his suit, a black baggy monstrosity made of heavy material to which age and many pressings had given a strange shine. Sitting opposite him, accepting one of his cigarettes, Christopher looked more closely at the sleeves of Bronski's suit. Indeed, there was a crease, and suddenly he had an image of the presser herself—a somewhat younger woman, mid-forties, wavy salt-and-pepper hair tied back to stay out of her eyes and away from the iron. Matronly but not a mother, kindly but not a crybaby, the presser of Jakob Bronski's suit came with it as a necessary evocation. Why? Because of the sleeves, because of what emerged from them— the hands. Certainly themselves incapable of manipulating an iron because on the left hand three fingers had been reduced to a row of uneven stubs, leaving the little finger, warped and curled towards the centre, as the only digit to oppose the thumb. Whereas on the right hand, the little finger was entirely missing, while the rest of the fingers were swollen, misshapen, scarred.

Bronski smoked, undid his tie, opened his jacket and rubbed his hands against his shirt and suspenders. A carafe of red wine appeared and Bronski was the one who reached out, grasped its neck in his huge palm, poured quickly into their glasses.

Then, still not having said a word, he ground out his cigarette, loosened his tie further and opened the top two buttons of his shirt. At the camp his collarbones had protruded, Christopher remembered, but now his neck was massive, accordioned by age, a thick muscular pedestal for the wide face with its deep oval canyons between cheekbones and jaw. Flat Slavic forehead with an unremembered mole over one temple. Thin white hair combed straight back. Eyes still slate green. Mouth unchanged. A fragile young man transformed into an old man who radiated size, authority, gravity.

And he had become a smoker, too. Or perhaps he had always been one but cigarettes were hard to come by at Drancy. In any case, now he smoked. In front of him were two packages of Peter Stuyvesant cigarettes. He was smoking them more or less one after the other, lighting them clumsily with wooden matches. Because of the matches and the cigarettes—or perhaps they were only the excuse—Bronski's hands were always in motion. Wrapping and unwrapping. Making flame or shaking it out. Moving his cigarette around in his mouth, from mouth to ashtray and back again; to say nothing of the constant raising of hands to pull at an ear, push an eyebrow into place, adjust suspenders, buttons, tie, press against the remains of the other hand.

All this, Christopher noted, and Bronski was still not talking. Just smoking, drinking, and eating now from the white porcelain bowls of olives that had been placed between them. Followed by platters of dolmades. Spiced chunks of lamb threaded by steel skewers. Steaming dishes of eggplant, tomatoes, peppers. Rice, cold pickled salads, a chicken cooked in lemon.

Jakob Bronski was holding his glass and looking across the table at Christopher. Since they had come into the restaurant something had been growing inside him. At first he had thought it was only one of those stones of grief that sometimes lodged in his chest and throat—as when he heard a certain kind of story, fended off a certain kind of memory. Those stones sometimes grew so large and so dense that he found himself choking, gasping for air, and could only relieve himself by punching his chest with his fist until it shattered.

In Christopher's face he could see the child easily enough. Remember him. The camp, yes: at least certain scenes, certain rooms, certain moments of pain that had been engraved too deeply to be removed. But then the hard currency of his memory had been debased, softened, made arbitrary by repeated applications of electricity to random sectors of the brain. What he had instead was an undernourished kaleidoscope, a partial jigsaw puzzle that could be reconstructed into more than one version—

His director had anticipated this problem. His director had encouraged him to understand that here was to be found ideological purity and free will: he had the ingredients for pictures both true and false—it was up to him, with the guidance of others, to will the true picture into place without yielding to the curiosity that was revisionism, the desire for hard currency that was historicism, the defeatism and bewilderment that were mental illness and would require more treatments—treatments that would on the one hand further inspire obedience but on the other make it more difficult to achieve.

Christopher was talking. Yes, it was pleasant to watch the child in his face, the eagerness to please, the boy who had always been able to charm his way in and out of every situation. Now the stone had heated up, come alive, begun to melt of its own accord.

Christopher's face was looming closer: alarmed, sympathetic, eyes peering into his. Jakob was frozen. Or at least he couldn't make the movements he wanted, whatever they would be, though he was in motion, vibrating, his knees knocking together, his arms beginning to shake so that the thick bottom of the glass stuttered against the table and sent a small tide of liquid sloshing over the rim.

The rain started shortly after they left the restaurant. Jakob Bronski looking, Christopher thought as he helped him into the taxi, absolutely forlorn, desperately unhappy. But once the taxi was moving Bronski smiled at him, put one of his maimed hands reassuringly on Christopher's shoulder, held his eyes in what could only be described as an embrace—a long and loving stare so unblinking, so warm with love, pain, the sweetness of late evening, that Christopher found his own tears rising, running down his face even as he pretended not to be crying, and went on, through his tears, accepting the cigarette Jakob offered him and setting it up in his mouth.

"Not so bad," Jakob said.

"Not worse."

"Could have been."

It was raining and the taxi's windows were closed. Jakob's clothes, Christopher noticed, smelled. Of sweat, of strong dry-cleaning fluid, of a cuisine that did not feature white sauce.

At the hotel Christopher went with Jakob to the front desk. Waited for him to get his key, then shook his hand and said goodnight.

"You've grown," Jakob said to Christopher as he was leaving.

"I'm fat now."

"You were always fat," Jakob Bronski was about to say. But then the picture of Christopher as a small cherub gave way to a gaunt and hollow-faced boy with a broken tooth. Or had that boy— "I almost remember you."

And then just as the stone was starting to grow again he saw Christopher's eyes swelling.

"Old men."

"Not so old," Christopher said.

"Sad men."

"Glad men."

III

## 1. How the Universe Began: The Big Bang, Part I

After we moved to the farm, the school bus picked me up in the morning and delivered me at the end of the afternoon. When my mother was home, our black Labrador, Adam, would be sprawled across the kitchen door, back pressed to the house's heat, white belly rotated to catch the sun. But when my mother was in town shopping with Ruth, Adam would lie at the top of the driveway where the car was usually parked, looking glumly down the road. As I came up the driveway Adam leapt forward, pushed the top of his skull into my hand while I walked up to the house. Where I would shut him out, leaving him to slump back into position across the door.

On one of those afternoons alone I found the NUMBERS file. My mother's files, her typing, the constant stream of letters to and from the house—these were familiar to me from before memory began. But I had never noticed the file with NUMBERS scrawled across the front in capital letters, my mother's herky-jerky printing that shot off at all angles like her arms when she broke into a dance.

She had left it on the kitchen table. It was an ordinary card-board folder time had turned a soft yellowy-brown.

I called out—there was no answer.

The afternoons I arrived at my parents' house to find it empty, just opening the door and breathing the air seemed dangerous. In the silence the ghosts of my parents' arguments echoed through the rooms. The way at night, as soon as we children were in bed, my mother's rages would begin; and against the drone of my father reasoning and pleading, her high broken voice would fly through the house like trapped birds.

First I had to go through all the rooms—not without bursts of fear that I would discover my mother hiding in a closet—and then, reassured, I made a final inspection of the downstairs and the counter where the mail was stored, before proceeding to the refrigerator. Nothing better than checking the house for ghosts, raiding the refrigerator and making a piece of toast for Adam, then going outside and sinking into the weather. Later, from the hills behind the house, I would hear the sound of my mother's car along the road. Then lie between the trees to watch the car as it crept up the driveway, my mother always peering anxiously through the windshield, as though her constant storms were bad weather making it impossible to see.

The afternoon I found the file I read it quickly, then fled outside. By the time my mother and Ruth got home, I was lying in my usual hiding place. Their coats were undone from the heat of the car. I was shivering against the frozen ground, my arm wrapped around Adam to keep him still and my free hand holding his nose to the leaves so he couldn't bark. But his tail was free, a bony black whip thumping against the ground like a partridge taking flight.

NUMBERS had been printed in wide black ink from a magic marker.

I opened it up. First I saw the two photographs. A line of children waiting to be served soup in front of a long table. The children had turned to the camera, most of them were smiling. One of the smiling girls, my mother later pointed herself out, had a tooth missing. She also later showed me Christopher Lewis at the end of the line, his face half hidden. He was wearing shorts, and from their bottoms extended legs so thin that the knees bulged out like swollen softballs.

The second picture was of Jakob Bronski. Of course I didn't know his name then; all I saw was a thin-faced man wearing a soiled white shirt. For some reason I thought he might be my grandfather.

The numbers themselves, and what they described, had been carefully written onto lined sheets of paper.

The day I found the NUMBERS file I was ten years old. My father arrived home a few minutes after my mother and Ruth. We were in the kitchen, silently looking at each other and the pages I had spread across the kitchen table.

My father took me by the hand and led me into the parlour. We sat down, my father and I. He reached for an atlas. "I should have told you this earlier. Your mother, when she was your age, spent two years of what should have been her childhood in a place called Drancy." He gave me a certain look, a professional quick-freeze to indicate he was moving from the role of father to that of eminent professor, arbiter-judge of time, history, mankind, etc. He must have used this look to vacuum in his various student admirers.

He gave me the look and then he said: "Drancy was a place outside a city called Paris. It was for—mostly—Jews." Again he paused. I remember the way he paused. I remember the way he looked at me. He was worried about me but I was feeling sorry for him. By rising to the bait of the file I had caused him to be conscripted for this duty I could see he had been avoiding. I was already promising myself that whatever he told me I wouldn't cry. To my surprise my father then announced: "We are Jews," as though this was news.

To help me understand his explanation, my father opened the atlas. He found a two-page spread of Europe and then proceeded to deliver the details—more or less—of the "extermination" of six million Jews. The registrations, the gatherings random and otherwise, the holding camps, the transportations to the death camps.

The day my father the eminent historian did his duty and turned those nightly rages into history itself—along with, I would later realize, him, me, Ruth and poor old Adam—I didn't want to know. "Ask any questions you like," he kept inviting me. As though, if I asked the right question, I could get the dirt back onto the gigantic cemetery he had just laid bare.

By the time my father had finished, it was dark. When we came into the kitchen my mother gave me her shy girlish smile and I started to cry. The only time she would ever get to see me crying over her.

## 2. Sooner or Later One of Us Must Know,
### or, The Strange Case of the Galaxy That Shrank:
### Estimated Number of Jews Wearing Yellow Stars
### when Paris Was Liberated: 20,000

I learned to like coming home to my parents' empty house. The ghosts, the echoes, the illegality of it all. But my mother came home to *her* parents' empty house only once. She would have been ten, the same age I was when I found the file.

The day my mother returned to that emptiness was in the month of October 1942. So she tells, but strangely doesn't remember the exact date. For over two years Paris had been occupied by the Third Reich—an occupation that had begun with polite German soldiers giving up their seats on buses to old ladies and wandering up and down the cobblestone hills of Montmartre gawking like every other tourist.

Now the first stage of the war—the traffic accident aspect, the humiliation, the shock, the possibility of thinking this occupation could be easily endured—was over. Of course there were some who prospered. Some who found the occupiers sympathetic. Some who had perhaps learned to put their hands in the pockets of the conquerors. So be it. Pockets exist to be emptied.

But there were also the inconveniences, the scary dark feelings, the slow shrinking of the city. The knowledge that what had once seemed a future without end was now simply a war like other wars. A war that would one day be over. With its victims and survivors. With its celebrations and reprisals. With its new dawn, its ghosts and its long shadows hanging over the future.

By May 1942 the tourist period was over, especially for the Jews. At first, believe it or not, the Jews in France couldn't imagine that the Germans had the same plans for them as for the German Jews. Even when the Jews of Paris—about a hundred thousand of them—were told to report to their local precincts, the vast majority complied. They must have believed that obeying the law would save them. This was, after all, France. The France of the French Revolution. The France in which the Revolution itself had proclaimed Jews might be full citizens of the new republic. Liberty, Equality, Fraternity.

By June 1942, the Jews were beginning to get the new message. Over 88,000 of them got it in the form of yellow stars—three each—to be worn in all circumstances; 88,000 yellow stars glowing in the City of Light.

By October 1942, 12,000 Parisian Jews had already been sent through Drancy to Auschwitz.

By October 1942, street arrests and random executions were commonplace. Jewish stores had been closed; Jewish lawyers had been rounded up and interned; a myriad of rules governing the wearers of yellow stars had been proclaimed. There were plans to conscript young French males for forced labour in Germany and across the city giant posters encouraged registration.

On the other hand Paris was still Paris. Every morning and afternoon children were swallowed up and then disgorged at the concrete mouths of the Métro stations. These stations were not quite so busy as they had been: flight, deportations and death had begun to pock the city. Apartments were unusually plentiful but food was difficult to get; and the eye found it hard to glide over various undesirable sights. On certain days the cafés served no alcohol except to men in German uniforms.

But Parisians still crowded in, if only to get warm. Even Jean-Paul Sartre had long ago walked away from the camp where he had been imprisoned after his capture at the beginning of the war. Now he was back teaching at his old school, writing the plays that would make him famous, seeing them produced on Parisian stages.

It was October 1942. A time, an era, a war that was no better or worse than many others. No reason for it to obsess me. No reason for me to hear those dying voices, those who died so long ago, when so many are dying today. But ever since I found my mother's NUMBERS file I've been circling around it, a morality play of which I can't quite grasp the whole lesson.

Even the arithmetic of death escapes me. Do the thousands who lived make up for the thousands who died? Of the thousands who died, should we subtract the number who would have perished in traffic accidents, flu epidemics, elevator failures, etc., during that same period?

If only half as many had died, would the war have been twice as good? Half as bad?

At an unknown hour on a day my mother is unable to remember, my mother's parents were picked up. They were Americans who had been caught in Paris. Bankers, Jews, small fry in the international world of finance sent to France for a year as part of some sort of exchange—more details about which my mother persists in being vague, or perhaps she never knew—Anyway, they were picked up.

Why?

Simple to explain, as my father used to say, just let go of my hand while I open the atlas and put you on a time machine to Drancy.

There you see Paris. And there, on its outskirts—today only a few minutes by Métro from the famous Luxembourg Gardens—was an apartment complex unfinished when Hitler's troops broke their long doldrums and pierced south into France, flowing by the Maginot Line as easily as—a few weeks later—they would parade in triumph down the Champs Élysées.

These apartments were arranged in the shape of a U. The three sides of the U each had six storeys of apartments. There were, of course, numerous halls and stairways connecting them. The authorities had intended this complex as a place to house the low-income families of Paris.

When the Germans came to Paris, they needed a temporary camp for French and Allied prisoners of war. Those unfinished apartments were perfect. And when the time came for Jews and other undesirables to be interned prior to being shipped off to their eventual destination, the POW camp was ready and waiting. The whole thing was organized by the French to please the Germans. Some say.

What kind of place did the new residents of Drancy find when they arrived? Noisy, chaotic, smelling of bad food, filthy clothes, constant and chronic epidemics of diarrhea. Children who had lost their parents and vice versa. Officials. Outside the gate the new arrivals had just passed through were often dozens of people: Red Cross workers, men and women searching for children or relatives, lawyers, police, soldiers.

Many, early on, didn't even know the name of the place to which they had been sent.

Drancy, it was called, after the neighbourhood. And then eventually Drancy-la-Juive, after the people who were kept there. Of the approximately 75,000 French Jews who were shipped by train to concentration camps—few of whom ever returned—67,000 came through Drancy, to be packed sometimes fifty or even a hundred to a room, bedded down in straw with a bucket for elimination. Drancy provided the ideal preparation for that final ride, and there were just under seventy such rides; the trains took, therefore, about a thousand passengers at a time.

Already you begin to see the problem: the trains, multi-car agglomerations of cattle cars and animal pens pulled by engines too decrepit for more important work, wait at the platform. Auschwitz, Birkenau, etc., etc., are meanwhile eager to receive.

But the trains from Drancy represent only a fraction of such trains traversing the continent at any given moment.

Imagine the continent as a body.

Imagine the death camps as its collective heart.

Imagine the train tracks as arteries and veins.

The heart beats, the heart needs something to pump, the heart yearns to consume.

At all times the vessels to the heart must be supplied.

Naturally, organization is not everything that it should be. A train sits at a platform. The times of its arrival and departure are known. Its destination is known. The destiny of its cargo is known. But where is the cargo? Who is going to fill up these trains?

It's fine, in the initial enthusiasm of submission, to volunteer a certain quota. But what happens when the easy ones have been sent, when the cream has been skimmed from the top, when a certain amount of disgust, resistance, other levels of difficulty have begun to make quotas difficult to fill? The heart begins to feel unloved.

And the camp itself, Drancy. Easy to say in retrospect that 67,000 passed through. But such things do not happen by themselves. It is not as if Drancy—a complex, yes, but still capable of holding only a few thousand at a time—could simply be filled up at the beginning and then gradually emptied through to the end. Although, in fact, during the last weeks alone—the last weeks before Liberation—thousands were shipped. On one convoy, only twenty days before Liberation, three hundred children were sent on a train. July 31, 1944. The invoices still exist. Every name was written down. But that convoy was accomplished only after a concerted roundup. As were the first shipments. In between, as was to be expected, were fat times and lean.

Fat times followed large operations, police sweeps of the officially listed residences of the 88,000 Parisian Jews who had not found a way to resist the obligatory registration. There were also the supplementary shipments through Drancy from other smaller camps spread around the country.

Lean times brought the problems of filling the train. Sometimes the heart had special needs in terms of able-bodied men and women. Sometimes the heart lost its appetite for children.

From the point of view of the heart, the hunger was constant. A heart has its needs. But out near the perimeters of the operation, out in the field, hunger is often appeased only on the run. Snatch and grab is sometimes the best you can do. Grab and gobble, as my mother said.

And so my mother's parents were grabbed. And gobbled. On that unknown October day of which my mother remembers the weather: "—sunny, a snappy wind, big leaves blowing in your face—"

## 3. Summary and Memory Work ... or, Nazi Krypton Rips Invisible Shield

14 June 1940: German occupation of Paris.
20 August 1941: Eleventh district of Paris is cordoned off and
   4,232 Jews are arrested.
3 October 1941: 7 synagogues in Paris are bombed.
27 March 1942: First deportation from Drancy (Paris) to
   Auschwitz.
   Mode of Transportation: 3rd class rail carriages.
   Contents of carriages: 1,112 Jews.
   Number who survived the war: 19.
   Special notes: this first convoy was the only one to use
   passenger carriages rather than freight cars.
16 July 1942: 12,884 Jews arrested by French police of which
   3,031 men
   5,802 women
   4,051 children.
   Special notes: # of suicides among those arrested: 106.

In her book of numbers my mother also noted that although
police had estimated, in May 1942, that over 100,000 Parisian
Jews were eligible to receive yellow stars, only 88,000 sets of

stars had been collected by the end of June 1942. Possible reasons for the gap: death, flight, lies, over-optimism of the authorities.

At the time of the German occupation, France was a secular state. Nowhere was it written—except voluntarily—who was a Jew and who was not. If your name, your accent, your nose, your passport, your neighbours, your relatives etc. were in order, who was to know better?

My mother's parents were Americans without affiliation to the French Jewish community. They did not register their religion with the police, nor did they collect yellow stars in the spring of 1942. They had been Jewish in America but in France they were not. As my mother explained to me, they only became Jewish again at the moment they were arrested.

Of course Melanie knew she was Jewish. But she knew also that it was something to be hidden. "With the other Americans," she would say, when a teacher or classmate asked where she went to church.

Even before the yellow star she learned to spot her fellow Jews on the street. Especially the foreign Jews: their shabby clothes, their accents, the way they tried to shrink into themselves—everything about them shrieked JEWISH REFUGEE. You could see their panic when the police appeared, demanding identity cards. Once she'd been in a store buying bread when a foreigner ran in, panting, sweating, eyes like an animal's, odours of fear spraying out of his thick coat. While everyone stayed in place, two policeman followed. My mother watched the eyes of the hunted man close, his face twist in shame, as the police grabbed him by the shoulders and led him away.

After the Jews of Paris had to start wearing the yellow star, my mother could see the same shamed faces on the marked Jews walking timid and humiliated along the sidewalks, sitting downcast and silent in the buses, lined up in front of stores for their allotted late-afternoon hour of shopping, crowded into the last car of the Métro. Signs were posted on the windows of stores owned by Jews; then the windows were shattered. Signs prohibiting Jews appeared in parks, theatres, even bathrooms. But pinned to the lining of her coat my mother had her invisible shield, her American passport.

Strangely, her parents had made no arrangements for her to go elsewhere in the event of their arrest. It had never occurred to them that they would be picked up; they were American foreigners in Paris. Enemy aliens, yes, but hostages for the thousands of Germans trapped in the United States. Despite the war there was, thus, this mutual non-obliteration pact. Registered they were, but as aliens, not Jews. Even their family name—Lansing (after the Michigan town where Melanie's grandparents had settled at the turn of the century)—was no giveaway. Although, in the end, they gave.

How could such a disaster have arrived? In fact, neither at the various death camps my mother later investigated nor at Drancy was there a record of her parents' names or internment. Perhaps they decided their American passports weren't good enough and were carrying other documents with other names. Perhaps the police identified them as part of some resistance cell and took them in for interrogation or simply to be shot. Perhaps—my mother sometimes wondered—they had for some reason panicked and fled, intending to come back and pick her up in a few hours or days.

No matter what the explanation, the fact is that on the morning of a day whose number is unremembered, my mother kissed her mother goodbye and set off with her father. They walked for two blocks, turned right, walked down another block to a traffic light. Crossed the street, continued for three blocks until they arrived at a plain grey building whose court was barred by a high spiked gate. It was a private school run by a Catholic order whose advantage was that they served lunch to the children. It also boasted a strong program in English studies, and my mother was often asked to read aloud so that the other children could hear and imitate her perfect American accent.

At the end of the afternoon, when the school gate opened, her mother wasn't there to meet her. She waited for a few minutes;

then, realizing that soon she would be conspicuously the last child, she set off alone.

At the apartment, no one came to open the door. Ten years old, my mother did not have her own key. There had never been occasion. She went down to ask the concierge if there was a message.

By the time I met Madame Brisot, one side of her face was hollow-cheeked where skin had gradually slid into the gap various teeth must have left. But she also showed me a different picture. The one I wanted to see: she, my mother, my grandparents, posed on the street, the nose of a big transport providing the backdrop. It must have been before the war. My mother looked — as in all her baby pictures — wiry and large-headed, with a wild mop of curls restrained by a ribbon. In the picture Madame Brisot's face had not yet been pulled out of shape — by missing teeth, by decades of insults, decisions made and possibly regretted. But that would be to accuse her. And in any case, my mother described Madame's face as kind, "a kind face, but she had sour breath."

Asked for a message, Madame Brisot did not reply right away. Melanie concentrated on her kind face. Madame Brisot accompanied her upstairs and unlocked the door. Everything was as it had been except that without her mother or father the rooms seemed much larger.

As it grew dark the rooms shrank again. Melanie sat in her usual chair without moving, waiting. When she had to go the bathroom she pressed her legs together until finally her knees grew so sore that she darted in, peed, then ran back to her chair.

Every time there were footsteps in the courtyard, voices, the sounds of someone climbing the stairs, her body began to unclench. Eventually, she stopped believing, and when the key turned in her lock she jumped up, startled.

Madame Brisot hesitated in the doorway and then held out her hand. Melanie ran to it. Clung to it as they descended.

Long after the war, long after my mother had become my mother, long after my father had told me what I wouldn't want to know, I went to Drancy.

You can get there by train from Paris—a short ride takes you to a concrete platform with yellow walls. The first time I went by. The second time I got off the train, climbed some steps. I should have brought a map. I must have thought there would be signs pointing to this historic monument. But when I walked along the street, a wide, bare suburban street much like any other, I found only a café.

I sat at a table by the window, drinking my beer, looking around for survivors old enough to blame. "I'm a Jew!" I could have shouted, but of course no one would have cared. It was, as they say, a dead issue.

Approximately 90,000 Jews spent time in Drancy during the war. Most were brought there in an organized way from various parts of France: some were picked up by police because they were caught without papers or reported by their neighbours; some even came there in search of missing children or parents. My mother wasn't even French. She was an American—ten years old—put in touch with the police by her concierge who either did or didn't know any better.

Those who did not starve to death in Drancy, or were not released, were sent to Auschwitz, where mostly they died. The day he explained my mother, my father told me all about the stone soap, the fillings, the mounds of skeletons.

Later, when I was in medical school, I came across my first book about the concentration camps. It was a volume of medical records a librarian had misfiled under "Internal Surgery". I stood in the library stacks, fascinated, trembling, flushed. I was twenty-two years old and had long lost my virginity, got drunk, taken drugs. I had dissected dead bodies, traded ridiculously obscene jokes, gone to bed with the wife of another man. But this was different. This was necro-pornography. Secrets about Jews, the torture of Jews, the humiliation of Jews. This was real people dying horrible deaths. My people. Had they not died, my life would have been different. I, my mother, my father, my sister — we would have been part of something impossibly good, something impossibly *reassuring* to be part of, something impossible for me to imagine. Had they not died there would be no Israel, no Occupied Territories, no gradual inevitable spiral towards the next disaster. But they did die. As they always have and always will until they are forgotten in the search for other victims. Leaving me, an irrelevant remnant of history, to remember their voices.

I smuggled the book out of the library, others like it, read them secretly in my room. Eyewitness accounts. Surgical experiments. Uprisings that were crushed. Pictures of living skeletons. Cadavers. A photograph of Jewish Polish seamstresses working in the Warsaw ghetto. Rows and rows of women: black hair pulled back, hopeful smiles, stitching for peace. And then the lens clicked and they were gone. Testimonials of survivors. Testimonials of non-survivors. Letters. Graduation certificates. Identity papers. Red Cross records. Statistics.

In the concentration camps was where the Jews had been killed. Although, when it was convenient or necessary, they had been killed elsewhere too. There were so many of them to dispose of. Drancy was at the edge of the nightmare, looking in. To get to the centre you had to take the train.

My mother didn't make that trip. Instead, at the end of the war, she was sent back to New England to live with her mother's relatives. To resume her life as a well-off American girl. To sing, to dance, to become beautiful and marry the eminent historian in order to become, finally, my mother.

**IV**

*1. Old Numbers*

Melanie listened to the running water. She was standing at the sink in the airport bathroom, cold water flowing over her wrists and hands. Down the drain; if she could be perfectly still, perfectly quiet, she knew she would hear the water working its way through the maze of airport pipes into the vast network of sewers bleeding the city's waste into the lake.

"Your body is your devil," a young man had whispered to her as they were coming into the airport. Dark beard, dead eyes, a silver amulet winking at her through the gap of an unbuttoned shirt. Benjamin had pulled her away.

Her fingers, her hands, her wrists grew numb. The hum and rumble of motors mixed with the swoosh of disappearing water.

She moved closer to the mirror. From her purse she took a razor blade, held it to the image of her face, between her eyes. Slice, a road of blood swelling out from the centre of her nose. She stared. But her hand hadn't moved. "You love your nose too much," she said to herself. Relaxed. Then in a quick movement she jerked the blade back, nicked one of her knuckles as though by mistake.

"Stupid bitch, who are you trying to fool?"

Julia had done her hands and hair; Ruth had gone downtown with her to buy a new suit, a light blue cotton that looked cheap in the fluorescent light.

Over the loudspeaker came a burst of static, then a sharp voice asking for baggage porters at the International Arrivals gate.

"International Arrivals gate," Melanie said aloud to herself. "Get there." She looked at her hands. They were back in the water, rigid again, stuck out like dead chicken feet ready to be popped into the soup. The cut on her knuckle was a pale pink mouth.

"Move," she said. Her hands drew back, rotated, searched for a towel in the dispenser. Then she took a bandage from her purse, wound it around her cut finger. "Hide your weapons, you idiot. Don't you know you can be dropped from the psycho-terrorist squad for self-mutilation, menopause or eating commercial doughnuts?"

The loudspeaker crackled again. Melanie saw her carefully composed face beginning to shimmer, as though it were a mirage preparing to disappear.

"Remember," Levin had told her, "you're not going to fall apart. Trust me."

"And if I do?"

"Call me." And, smiling at the absurdity of his own promise, he'd pushed a coin into her hand.

Now Melanie felt for that coin in her pocket, squeezed it until the edges bit into her palm. The reflection of her face grew quiet. In the mirror she saw a middle-aged woman, well preserved, a bit stiff, gathering courage in the airport bathroom.

She was leaning into Benjamin when Bronski came out. For a moment she could only watch him moving forward, wide shoulders curved with the weight of his suitcases. Behind him was Christopher, baby-faced and beaming, long silvery hair hanging in a half-circle about his shoulders.

"There they are." Benjamin took Jakob's suitcases, then Melanie stepped to him and Jakob's arms were around her. Her face pressed into his jacket. Sweat, smoke, an old smell, Bronski's smell, the ripe off-centre odour of his shirt she'd wallowed in the last time he'd hugged her. That was just before he left for Auschwitz. Her face had only reached his chest then and he'd held her so hard her nose had been squashed. And the smell ground into it so that for weeks after she found herself thinking that he'd miraculously reappeared, that if she reached out in the dark he'd be there, watching her sleep.

With Christopher it was his big hands on her shoulders, a delicate peck on the cheek, before he held her at arm's length, appraising.

"You're looking great."

"Liar," Melanie said. She felt herself beginning to blush, which was ridiculous, and to cry, which was natural, and it was Jakob who comforted her while she cried, unable to stop until finally Jakob extracted a hankerchief so grey and wrinkled that they all started to laugh.

The men insisted on food before leaving the airport. Christopher and Benjamin were dispatched to take the suitcases to the car; Melanie was left with Jakob in the cafeteria.

His voice over the telephone from Paris had sounded strong, youthful, even more forceful than she had remembered it. And now his size—the bones, the muscles, slabs of flesh like layers of lava. The fires poor Jakob must have burned in. "To tell you the truth," Christopher had admitted on the telephone—"I even wondered if there had been—"

"A switch?"

"A switch. A hitch."

Of course she had also thought of that. Long ago, when she had first started corresponding with the man who called himself Bronski. True, the photograph had set her off, but the tone of the letters themselves, their strange formality, the lack of any real reference to details at the camp. The guts, the smell, the deep-down lock they'd had on each other, were missing. But she hadn't cared: if she was sending her food, her books, her love to the wrong man—an impostor Bronski stranded in a Moscow mental home with false papers—well, even impostors need to eat.

"Tired?"

Bronski shrugged and smiled. She watched his hands as he took out a package, shook free a cigarette, lit it.

"What happened?"

"Accidents."

"Working?"

"Night work. Do they make you afraid?"

"I am afraid. Not of your hands but—" *Night work.* They had been locked after all. *Night work.* The words tumbled uncomfortably in her mind.

"But?"

He had written her to say that the man who lived with him, took care of him, had finally received an exit visa and was going to Israel; that he too had been offered such a visa but wasn't sure where he wanted to go. Come here, Melanie had replied. Not believing it could happen.

His face was broad where it had once been hollow, the thick black hair she remembered tumbling forward was now thinner, mostly white, pushed straight back. But suddenly a strand fell down, over his forehead, and a smile began. And then she remembered his lips used to tremble before he smiled, as though unsure whether to laugh or cry. Now they were quivering the same way.

"God," Melanie said. Her breath caught in her throat. She reached out for Jakob's hands. They were rough, broken. Folds of flesh melted together. A bombed-out city of jagged buildings, stumps, craters. She realized she was digging her nails into his scars. "Sorry, I just—I'm supposed to be taking my medicine— but for the first time I wanted to see you without it. Do you mind?" Warmth was running through her fingers, her palms, up her arms—as though from his reopened wounds his blood was flowing onto her. "Me too," she said, showing him her bandaged finger. "Aren't I disgusting?" Nearby a chair scraped across the floor. At the camp the rats had sometimes squealed in the night, and waking up she had always been sure those squeals were the sounds of teeth scraping bone. Fear invaded her now, all at once, a blitzkrieg of panic. She was squeezing Jakob's hands, what was left of them, squeezing them the way she used to, squeezing them with all her strength. At the camp she had learned to be silent. Inside, no. Inside was a perpetual clamour of fear, rumblings of trains and trucks setting out for unknown destinations. Unable to move, unable to breathe, unable to stop listening, unable to shift her eyes from the immobile face of Jakob Bronski which now, melting under her stare, began sliding back and forth from the young man she had known to the old man he had become. Bronski was breathing hard, almost groaning, breathing hard and slow and staring at her the way he used to when she was so frightened that he had to breathe for both of them, so frightened that she would squeeze his hands and hold her breath hoping that she could die now, die in safety, die and be taken away from the death she couldn't bear. Melanie felt the tears starting.

Bronski's lips were quivering. "Breathe," he used to say. "Breathe," in a voice so soft it could be felt but not heard. His lips were quivering and she was weeping but Melanie knew he wouldn't cry with her because he never did.

"Please," Bronski said.

"Don't worry, I won't crack up. I mean I already have. I just wanted to see you, the first time. I can handle it." Her arms were sore and the muscles of her back were sending out their own calls of pain. When she had started to make love with men she had found herself squeezing the same way, unable to help herself, clawing into the back of her frightened lovers until one day she saw the bruises her fingers had made. Now she forced her lungs to push in and out. A few weeks ago, the one man she'd had an affair with—but years ago—a one-night disaster followed by a series of what he called "friendship dinners"—had tracked her down on the telephone.

Said he'd heard she'd been having problems but he had too, could they see each other again. When she refused, he started to ramble, as though he was in his own nuthouse somewhere, pumped full of his own life-enhancing drugs. "You have great tits and a perfect smile," he finally told her.

"You're out of date," she replied, amazed to hear her long-lost college-girl voice straining to come back with a smart remark. Now she had control of her hands again: she lifted them away from Jakob and wiped at her cheeks.

"You turned into a beautiful woman," Bronski said.

"No."

"Yes. Inside, too. You are very brave and very beautiful."

"I'm not beautiful inside. Believe me."

"No."

"Inside I'm— Don't you think something was done to us—" But then she stopped, wondering how she could be saying this to, of all people, Jakob Bronski, how she could say that the camp had destroyed her and made her ugly when he had survived, lived through, failed to survive, so much more, so much worse. Or perhaps that wasn't the point.

Jakob took his hands away, reached for his cigarettes, offered one to Melanie.

"No thanks."

"People don't smoke here? I heard that."

"Some people smoke. I smoke sometimes."

"Afraid of cancer?"

Melanie had stopped crying. She took out a cigarette, put it between Jakob's lips. "Here you can smoke, you can drink, you can chase the girl next door." She reached into her purse for her lighter, the gold initialled one David had given her on their first anniversary. MLW: Melanie Lansing Winters. Melanie Lancing Splinters.

"America," Jakob sighed.

"Canada."

"And there is a difference?"

"Of course."

"But you were an American when we met."

"I moved to Canada to be with David."

"But living in Canada has not made you beautiful inside? Why did you bring me here?"

When he laughed the skin of his face pulled back and his fleshy nose went suddenly narrow, the narrow beaky nose of the young man who had searched her out the first day at Drancy and told her that he was hoping that they would both live for at least a week, since he was counting on learning English from her—

He had stopped laughing and was starting to cough. His face turned scarlet. Then one of his giant fists rose from the table, drove like a hammer into his chest.

There was a final eruption, the sound of something deep dislodged. Then he started breathing again.

"Don't die here."

"I promise." He ground out his cigarette and the scraping of its paper against the glass ashtray made the hairs on her arms tingle. She listened to him breathe, made her own breathing match his.

"I'm a stupid bitch, Jakob. I wanted everything to be right for you and now I'm falling apart."

"You always said that, Melanie. But you're the one who held us together."

He was leaning forward. She was losing herself in his eyes, the new lines around his mouth, the way his lips shaped themselves carefully with each word.

She realized she was squeezing Levin's coin. Levin's currency. If she squeezed hard enough she would become Levin's patient again. MLW: Melanie Lansing Winters, Melanie's Dancing Dinners—ex-smoker, ex-eater, ex-camp victim, ex-wife, ex-mother, ex-psycho-terrorist, X-marks-the-spot for a woman who had done nothing but learn to go to the very bottom and bounce up again. Nothing but.

"You always held us together," Jakob repeated.

"Listen to what people tell you about yourself," Levin had advised her.

She was listening and Jakob was talking. From the very first day at the camp he had insisted on talking to her, talking to her in his English which was so bad she couldn't understand him. "You supply the missing words," he had instructed. Sometimes almost all of the words were missing. Not now. She tried to concentrate on what he was saying. Something about the time a guard had tried to hit Christopher and she had gone insane with rage, screaming and clawing until Jakob had been able to pull her off.

"You made them respect you," he was saying now. "No one else would have dared."

"And you learned English. You speak so well now."

"My friend in Moscow—the man who took care of me before he went to Israel. He had spent ten years in London and we practised together. You should have heard us at night, whispering our lessons. 'Would you like some tea?' 'Rather, yes. Milk and sugar please. And don't forget the toast.' "

"He wasn't learning Hebrew?"

"That too. Sometimes we even read the Bible. We noticed, for example, that in the story of my namesake there was no mention of going to synagogue. When God had something to say, He appeared in person."

She was about to ask if they also prayed together, as she had, that everything would work out—but her mouth was paralysed in a smile she couldn't remove, so she just nodded her head, hoping he would get the idea.

## 2. The Enigma of Arrival

It was a week since Levin had brought Melanie home from Heritage Acres. She had crossed the lawn, walking loosely, casting her unsettled aura, swinging her eyes back and forth as though they were radar guns. "Hello, David." The new miracle drug Levin had found for her lowered her voice and gave it a dangerous subterranean crackle. "Are you going to offer us tea, or what?" *Or what?* With Melanie there was always that loose end, that illogical dangling string inviting you—daring you—to go past the surface. But into what? Thirty years ago he had thought she was the challenge he needed, a chance to dive below the surface of pretend emotions to something deeper, a truer level of emotional reality. "Or what?" he would have answered. Now he went for the kettle.

Once, drunk, several years after the passionate period of their relationship had ended, David had tried to write her a letter. This had taken all night, a night he spent alone at the farm during one of those weeks he came to cut wood. The letter explained he could no longer be with her because they were living on two different planets. Her planet was composed of mass graves, cemeteries, prisons. To her, the pleasures and trials of everyday life were merely a veneer to cover over the gaping sores of history, man's infinite capacity for evil, the true cities of man which were suffering and death. When she dreamed at night, for example, she often moaned and cried—and if in the midst of a dreamless moment the house was shaken by a passing truck or streetcar, she would wake up, clutching him, to warn of an earthquake or falling bombs. Such a vision, he had said, seemed unreasonable to him. And anyway, why worry about the whole world when there were welfare bums and winos passed out and freezing to death all around them? Starving and illiterate children renting the holes in their bodies for drugs? Natives encysted on reserves in their own country? Why should one person's suffering be more important than the suffering of another? But although he had continued in this line for over two hours, he had been incapable of moving on to the next step, the step he had to arrive at. Which was his own dreams. But his own dreams were not about these alternate, closer-to-home injustices. His own dreams, in this epoch, had been strictly of the flesh. Every night he dreamed he was in bed with a different young woman. These dreams—so real, so satisfying, so complex and gentle and absolutely human—these dreams gripped him so strongly that for several months he felt the only purpose of being awake during the day was to keep himself healthy enough to sleep deeply at night.

He had signed the letter "with respect and admiration, David." These words had seemed just what was required: cold, final, elegiac. Then he'd poured himself a coffee and a shot of brandy. A few swallows later, he realized that if he left Melanie it would only be to seek out someone else. Another woman to betray and desert in favour of a yet more unknown female phantom. Why bother? he'd asked himself. Faced with this final unanswerable question he threw the letter in the fire.

The stroke had happened on his seventieth birthday. That day David had taught his usual classes, then gone for a walk across the campus. The afternoon was cold but clear. Sky a crackling winter blue, newly frozen ground carpeted with golden leaves, bare-branched trees extending upwards like rifle-shots. After his walk he had come home and treated himself to a sherry in front of the fire. The wood was birch, chunks from a fallen tree he had felled and split more than a year ago. September then. Melanie in the kitchen, typing letters to the imprisoned of the world, while he thought of nothing but the sun reflecting off the bleached pine of the woodshed, his narrow whippet body stripped to the waist and sweating as he wielded the axe.

On the afternoon of his seventieth birthday he had the house to himself. Mozart, spitting flames, sherry, an imported cigar—small pleasures that still pleased.

"Seventy," he had said aloud. It was an amazing thought. Amazing grace. Followed by a comic-book explosion—BAM!!—a jagged fissure of terror ripping open the careful surface of his afternoon. His jaw dropped, the muscles of his face went slack. He was unable to move, even to sit down. Then the ground sealed over; he was standing in front of the fire staring at a knot in a birch log, a knot from which beaded pearls of thick sap were dropping into the flames.

Melanie came home. He said nothing. He was seventy, Melanie over fifteen years younger.

That night he had gone to bed happy. Not drunk, but tired. Content to find himself between warm clean sheets with Melanie's body cupped around his, Melanie's hands massaging his back, Melanie's breath on his neck as she held him the way she used to. The panic hadn't come back that evening. He had felt not fearful but rich, sentimental, boringly joyous at the tolling of his threescore and ten.

Then, lying still, eyes closed, he heard the crackle of lightning again. Electricity on the loose. Electricity leaking from somewhere, needing somewhere to go. He remembered that—the vision of himself as a power station, a series of overloaded circuits. The next memory was hospital.

In the hospital, sedated, he had passed the time with his eyes closed, pretending he was at the farm. Now he was on his feet again. Standing in the middle of the room that had once been the ground floor of the horse barn, complete with elm-framed stalls and galvanized iron troughs. Leaning on a heavy square-hewn post, David found his hands sliding over the axe scars. When he first moved to the farm, David Winters, dizzy with born-again rural fervour, had cleaned and reconsecrated this barn. Later Benjamin—his son, Timmy's father—had helped him carry water to the troughs and load hay into the loft above so that on frosty winter mornings the bales could be dropped to the horses waiting below.

After the horses had been sold, the barn entered a new incarnation. The doors were replaced by large windows; the cement floors covered with insulation, plywood, carpeting; the walls panelled with barnboard salvaged from a building that had collapsed during a hurricane.

"Is he coming here to die?"

The sound of his grandson's voice startled David. For a moment he lost his balance and had to steady himself on the post. "Is he coming here to die?" Timmy asked again and David suddenly wondered if Timmy was used to this kind of repetition.

"Who?"

"That Russian."

"He's coming here to get strong," David said. *Here* being Canada, or more exactly—and with Timmy's seven-year-old mind exactness was everything—the farm David had bought with Melanie almost thirty years ago.

"Does he know anything about dinosaurs?"

"He *is* a dinosaur," David said. Then, seeing the look on Timmy's face: "Not really. But the other man knows about dinosaurs. A long time ago your grandmother and I went to the desert with him and dug for old bones."

David watched his grandson slide onto the bench and begin pecking at the keys of the piano. A children's song David recognized but couldn't name emerged in fits and starts.

Melanie had bought that piano for a hundred dollars from the the MacFarlanes, once the neighbours down the road. Ancestral MacFarlanes had been the first to settle this tiny valley: the week after the bank threatened to foreclose, they put their furniture on

the lawn and auctioned off everything: house, pets, machines—
"A hundred dollars!" David had complained when Melanie told
him how much she had paid. That was after she had come back
from her first breakdown and he couldn't help testing her as
though she were a car fixed by an unlicensed mechanic.

David began opening the windows. New breezes, bird and insect sounds, the thick twinned odours of hay and clover, swept
inside. Until finally David—still listening as Timmy launched
once more into his song—found himself thinking, not for the
first time, that when this room was full of outside air, all the furniture and trimmings clean, everything arranged to perfection,
it was still not so satisfying as it had been when it was still a barn
and he could walk the cement floor in his hard-soled workboots.

The piano had stopped and he was aware of Timmy observing him. His look was curious and speculative, like his high
voice when he asked about the prospective lifespans of various grandparents and neighbours. He could be wondering if
I'm about to fall on my face, David thought. A possibility, to be
sure, although it hadn't happened yet. In fact, despite his stroke
he felt remarkably fit, the old bones and muscles still ready
for a day of sawing and cutting wood, puttering at carpentry,
walking over roads and fields.

Timmy had come up to him and taken his hand.

"Do you want to go looking for frogs?"

David hesitated. "I might. You go back to the house and I'll
come to get you."

"Soon?"

"Soon." The boy's voice tugged at him. His face, his eagerness. What you really need is to go looking for frogs with
your father, David almost said. There had been a time when
he made various remarks about Benjamin—to Timmy, to Helen,
to Melanie, to Benjamin himself. Sharp remarks, little twisting
cuts he thought might get Benjamin moving along the road he
was supposed to follow. Any road. Although collecting frogs
was not something—along with all other such activities—he
had ever done with Benjamin. He had his hands open on his lap

and was staring at his palms. They were wrinkled, lined, irregularly callused and bumped. There was a scar that had been made
by a fish-hook. And the hot weather had swollen his fingers. He
didn't want to go collecting frogs with Timmy. And he didn't
want to worry about Benjamin. He just wanted to be in the centre of himself. He just wanted to sit in this chair and think about
how much better the barn had been when there was no chair to
sit in. He wanted to think about Melanie's return to the farm,
about the way her presence dug at his nerves now, just as it had
for more than thirty years, about how much he hated the sensation of that digging, about all the injuries it had caused him
to do her during their marriage, the thousand and one revenges
with which—unable to stop himself—he had tried to undermine
her the way she tunnelled beneath his own carefully constructed
trenches and fortifications. Trench warfare, yes, that was what
their marriage had been. Decade after decade he had won the
decisive battles; but in the end he had only worn himself down
to the point where his own grandson was waiting for him to die
while Melanie, on the rebound once more, was still young, still
beautiful, still capable of surrounding herself with allies.

He sat down at the piano and played a slow scale. The notes
were hollow and out of tune. Before Melanie—in a fit of spite—
had demanded it be exiled to the barn, the piano used to be in
the parlour. While Benjamin and Ruth were at school, she would
practise her songs for the dance classes. While he, usually within
hearing, played at being the gentleman farmer. Once, when he
was digging postholes for a fence to separate the barnyard from
the lawn, the ridiculous tinkling sound of her playing bored its
way so deep into his brain that he ran into the house screaming
at her until his throat was sore and his face was covered with
sweat.

Through one of the openings where hay used to be dropped
down to the horses, stairs now led to the loft. David himself
had built this stairway, using thick pine planks bought from
a nearby mill. The mill was closed now, the radial arm saw
he had used was on permanent loan to a neighbour who had

started a woodworking shop. But the stairs, David noted with satisfaction, still welcomed each footstep with a solid *thunk*.

In the loft he found himself opening windows again. Soon Christopher would be here. Looking about in his mocking way, bursting with unbelievable enthusiasm, making David feel as though he were a highly trained dog, a savage on a leash, a rustic hewer of wood who had to be treated with good-natured friendliness lest he turn his axe on his foreign guest. Or perhaps that wasn't fair, David admitted. Perhaps Christopher was no longer, even never had been, in love with Melanie or jealous of him.

But the book, *Ape Man*, had been pure provocation. Bad enough to have used his friends to make a novel, to have used their romance for the novel's romance, but the sex scenes between the narrator, Christopher—thinly disguised—and Melanie—thinly clothed—were nothing but an embarrassing public wet dream.

On the mattress was the bedding Melanie had prepared for Christopher. David made the bed, hands smoothing the carefully ironed linen, lifting the mattress to secure the corners of the sheets. And then, not looking back, he went downstairs and out onto the lawn that joined barn to house. Midday heat, the buzzing of flies, the deep dizzying greens of grass, leaves, hedges, shrubs, swimming towards the naked sun.

He crossed the lawn, towards not the house but the cowbarn, the largest building on the property and still in use.

Inside the barn was dark and cool. Although the doctors had forbidden it, he picked up the wide-bladed shovel and pushed it slowly up and down the centre alley. As he worked he began to sweat; soon he could feel the wet back of his cotton shirt sticking to his skin. It was a good feeling and he kept working, enjoying the smell of hay and manure, the hard feel of the floor beneath his shoes, the rhythm of moving first into darkness, then towards the blue light at the door.

When the aisle was cleared he put away the shovel and took up a pitchfork. When they had just moved to the farm, when the myth was reality, when the children were in school and Melanie was still anchored in herself—or at least apparently anchored in the self he had believed her to be—then he had loved these hours in the barn testing his muscles against the needs of the cattle, cleaning, feeding, respecting the laws of a universe of heavy animals and big-beamed buildings.

With the pitchfork he turned the straw in the first stall. That was the stall that belonged to Juliet; she was the Queen Cow, the mother-in-chief, the favourite target of a bull so amorous that everyone within ten miles knew him as Romeo.

Now he could feel his breath coming harder. David set the pitchfork down. He was leaning against the post of Juliet's stall. When he was a child in Toronto, he had carved the name of a now-forgotten girl into the top of his desk. Which had caused him—for the first and only time in his life—to be strapped. Now, for some reason, he could feel the satisfying give of the wood beneath his knife blade. A knife blade not so different from the one in the penknife he now took out, opened, and began using on Juliet's stall. J-U-L-I-E-T. One after another the letters formed. And as the wood splintered, he could smell the newly exposed cedar, raw and pink. J-U-L-I-E-T. Like the television program that used to come on after the hockey game, starring "Our Pet, Juliette". In that honeymoon period on the farm, they had once gone to their neighbour's for supper; on the way out to the car they saw a bull climbing over a cow. The dinner had been a celebration which featured a very alcoholic punch. That night after the children were in bed, Melanie, drunk, had turned to David in the kitchen and told him to come upstairs. Carrying the bottle of brandy with her—the signal she sometimes gave. Then asked him to mount her from behind, like that bull.

Standing in the barn, his chest easing, he could hear Melanie's hoarse voice, the surprisingly heavy grunt that had escaped her when she got what she wanted and—after a moment of shocked silence—had started them both laughing.

He walked away from it, out of the barn, around the back so he could be shaded.

By the time he got to the house he was exhausted. Helen was at the kitchen counter, listening to the radio and chopping vegetables for one of the tubs of green tomato relish she made every summer. Some years, when in the evening the air in the kitchen was heavy with the smells of simmering tomatoes, onions, herbs, David had stayed up late drinking with his daughter-in-law and former student, comfortably nursing what would once have been a flicker of desire until the clock chimed midnight and he stepped out to "check the animals"—code for walking barefoot across the cool dewy grass and peeing beside the lilac bush at the driveway's edge.

"Timmy went to play at the Spencers'," Helen said. "And Benjamin called from the highway. He said they'd be here in two hours."

In his graduate seminar on "the morality of war", she had been light-years ahead of the others; two years working in Africa had left her articulate, cynical, filled with an uncomfortable mixture of hope and anger. Dark and wiry, her narrow face a bit too concentrated to be beautiful, she had kept her looks; but a decade of Benjamin, Timmy, combining the duties of work and home, seemed to have sedated her.

Melanie's desk was at the back of the kitchen, in a bay window looking out to the back garden. On top of her portable typewriter was a thick sheaf of papers. Since she had come back to the farm to wait for Jakob Bronski, she spent hours every day pounding out her missives to dictators, presidents, prime ministers, demanding the release of long lists of unjustly detained and tortured prisoners.

There was also, on the desk, a small stack of letters already arrived for Jakob Bronski: one from the sainted Rabbi Goldman; several with the logo of the Canadian Jewish Congress; one with his name simply handwritten on the front and PERSONAL printed beside it.

"The labours of justice," David muttered.

"What?"

"Nothing. I was wondering how Melanie is doing."

"I think she's fine," Helen said with her back to him. "I really think she's going to be all right. Do you remember the way her fingernails used to be? Bitten right down to the knuckle. Now she has beautiful hands. Levin said the whole thing might have been a hormone problem caused by malnutrition at the camp."

"Menopause," David said, and regretted it right away.

This time Helen did turn to him. "I've always wondered why she kept coming back to you." Then she stopped and put her hand on his chest. "You picked a bad century to be born a man. Don't be so hard on yourself."

She stood for a moment and it was David, not wanting her to see him soften, who looked away.

## 3. Elementary Functions,
### or, Mother Steps Out, Part I

Melanie opened the car door for Christopher, then walked around to the driver's side. This afternoon she had been a good girl. At lunch, after getting back from the airport, she had spilled her pills onto the table, ostentatiously counting them out. "See what a devoted wife I am?" she said to David after she swallowed—then realized that in fact these might have been the first words she had spoken directly to him for days. As Levin had explained to her: "You need those pills, but the pills aren't in control—you are." When the medicine was in her, the prescribed dose securely in her blood, anchoring the stray sheep, she could believe that story. When she was taking the pills she *did* feel in control. With the pills she could look at faraway trees on the horizon, listen to the birds, watch the edges of things move slowly and smoothly into each other. With the pills she could be herself, Levin said, and she would have believed him except that without them she felt another self emerge, her real self. At first a sharp, focused seer, a magician-clairvoyant to whom love, anger, desire were as visible as weather. Until the weather grew stormy, as it always did, and she drowned.

As Christopher settled himself in the passenger seat, she looked up to the house. No one was watching. When the dishes were done and Jakob had gone upstairs for a nap she had told David that Christopher was coming to town with her to shop. David, sitting at the kitchen table with chequebook and a stack of bills, had only nodded. Now Christopher was smiling at her. In the dozen years since she had last seen him, time in the form of lines, wrinkles and sags had invaded his smooth babyface and turned it three-dimensional. "You look more human with wrinkles," she imagined herself saying. She realized she was staring at his face, sinking into the idea that a new, empathetic and compassionate Christopher had emerged from the brittle author of *Ape Man*. Or maybe only the face was different and inside he was still smooth, the same old impervious Christopher trying to soak up the details but getting them all wrong; and then in a year or five they would reappear in a new novel for David to curse and throw across the room.

She began backing down the driveway. It was so long since she had been this close to Christopher. His large hips and shoulders threatened to overflow the passenger seat of her Honda, and when she reached down to shift gears her arm lay against his.

"Good to see you," Christopher said.

Without thinking she drew her arm away. Then, self-consciously, moved her hand again, this time to lay it against his cheek. Even while she was stroking his wispy sideburn, once more hypnotised by his transformed face, she was aware of David in the farmhouse, of the row of trees curtaining off the window through which he might be watching.

Melanie slid her hand back to the gearshift, accelerated, felt the wheels spin on the gravel as the car fishtailed briefly, then accelerated up the hill towards the highway.

So good to be out of Stalag Estomac. On the loose. Driving about as though her little intermissions—this latest almost a year—didn't exist. A song was running through her mind, a western song she had heard with Helen the other day. They had been sitting opposite each other at the table, chopping the ends off beans, then stuffing them into freezer bags, when they discovered they had both stopped working to listen to the story of a woman who got into her car with the man she wanted to be her lover but couldn't tell, then put her foot on the gas pedal and drove along a highway into the setting sun until she reached a bridge. A high-flying crying soprano bridge that carried her car out into the middle of nowhere—then left her crying and flying down down down through the air into the water, singing the whole time and dreaming that they were flying to the promised land.

Now she tried to imagine how it might feel if Christopher were her lover and they were driving away from the farm for ever and into the sunset. Except that she had never made love to Christopher, never in a million years would have made love to the old smooth Christopher; and squinting out the window at the dusty road she was biting her cheeks to keep from laughing at the thought of Christopher's big stone-white stone-smooth belly lying on her small crumpled one.

At the curve near the dump she slowed. Somehow, just thinking of Christopher as a lover had made something change. Like trying on a new dress or a new drug. The colours or the smell of the dust.

When she came to the highway she played the tourist guide, pointing out the various farms to Christopher, telling him the names of the people who lived there, the scandals for which they were locally known, the times they had helped David or vice versa. As she talked she could hear her voice pocking, little empty spots of nervousness, little bearpits of nothing you had to skip over or else you were gone, like that woman, down down down.

In the rearview mirror her face looked strong and solid: high cheeks flushed with the sun, thick hair parted in the middle. But out at the edges something was beginning to happen, a blur: then Christopher's arm flashed in front of her; the heel of his hand hit the steering wheel and sent the car skidding across the road, almost into the ditch before he pulled it back again.

Melanie jumped out of the car, ran to where the girl lay at the side of the road, her legs tangled up in her bicycle. Seeing Melanie she stood up to show she wasn't hurt. "My God, I didn't see you—"

"I'm all right." The girl was squinting into the sun. One of her knees had been scraped on the gravel and her bicycle chain had come off. While Christopher fixed the chain Melanie rubbed the girl's leg clean with a piece of Kleenex.

"I didn't even see you. If Christopher hadn't—"

"I'm all right—please—"

They put the bicycle in the trunk. Christopher squeezed into the back while the girl—her name was Valerie Stenton—gave Melanie directions. Sandy hair, freckles, a soft bony face. Her mother was a schoolteacher, her father an insurance executive in Kingston.

"You're Melanie Winters," Mrs. Stenton said when Melanie introduced herself, as though to tell Melanie she knew everything, *everything*. "And I'm Gloria, even the *children* call me Gloria." She insisted on making coffee and blaming the whole accident on her daughter. "I tell you, she should watch where she's going on that thing."

They drank their coffee outside, on the deck that joined the house to the backyard swimming pool. Beyond the yard was a field, treeless save for one huge beech. A cluster of cows lay in its shade, their slowly nodding heads surrounded by flies.

By the time they had finished the coffee and sampled date squares from the local bakery, they had talked about the school and established that Mrs. Stenton had started teaching two years after Benjamin left, but while Ruth was still there.

"Your daughter won the spelling one year," she now remembered. She looked up into the sky, as though Ruth's victory were there to be seen, etched into the heavens.

Melanie nodded. She felt wrong. Gloria Stenton was wearing lipstick, a print dress unbuttoned to show the top of her brassiere and a narrow line of untanned skin. She looked, Melanie thought, like a high-class waitress in one of those pizza places where Levin sometimes took her. Her own clothes made her feel fat and old. With Gloria Stenton, getting sun-fried on the bare deck, she wished she were like driftwood, narrow, hard and polished.

"You used to be on the parents-teachers," Gloria Stenton said.

" 'She used to be on the parents-teachers,' " Melanie said to Christopher when they were back in the car. " 'I hear she's in a home now.' " Her voice folded around the flat local tones. " 'We were going to visit her, if we ever got down to Toronto. Do you suppose she'd even remember us? I guess she isn't that far gone. Well, tell her hello, anyway. I was going to knit her something but Betty—she'll remember *Betty*—had twins and then she needed help with the canning—' "

" 'In a home,' " Christopher took up.

" 'They tell me.' " She had the voice perfectly now. Why not? It had grown into her, year by year: the flat voice and, she supposed, the equally flat uninterested gaze with which the locals surveyed her as she made her purchases at the stores, used the post office to mail her packets of letters to foreign countries. " 'They tell me she went crazy when her husband started fooling around. She was always a bit—you know—she had a dancing school in Kingston for a while, can you believe it? The husband ran off with one of the teachers, she was top-heavy, you know what I mean? But she came back to him, always does when she gets out of the nuthouse. You can see her in the liquor store every Saturday morning, yup.' "

Christopher was laughing. "I don't believe you—"

" 'Yup, it's true. Every Saturday morning like clockwork. Two bottles of gin and two bottles of red wine. Least that's what Willy says, I never saw her myself because she sneaks in early so as no one would see her, yup, after a week of being nuts you gotta get oiled. And it's not just drinking. The other day I saw her driving around with a foreigner. Don't know what they were up to but they ran over the Stenton girl on her bicycle, yup. Then she brought her friend right into the Stenton house. He was a foreigner. Didn't even know enough to sit and wait in the car. Course Gloria, you know Gloria, she would never say anything. Just made them a cup of coffee and watched them eat up all the date squares. They must have thought she owned the bakery—' " Talking made her feel better, relaxed; the incident with the girl had faded but the song was still running in a corner of her mind.

Windows open, sun pouring in, they had pulled up at the bakery itself, a small converted house located right beside the supermarket.

"You hate it here," Christopher said.

"Not really."

She turned to Christopher. The black seatbelt made a wide arc across his sloping belly, pressed into the shoulder of his polo shirt and pulled the neck slightly sideways. Along the bridge of his nose, in the corners of his eyes, beaded along his forehead, were tiny drops of sweat. It was odd how he sweated: such a big man, such tiny drops of sweat. A darker larger stain of sweat had formed on his shirt about his belly.

The sun was coming in so brightly she could see patchy areas where his shave had not been close. A thin line of silvery hairs just beneath his jaw.

"I'm trying to imagine you with a beard."

"I had a beard once. It made me look like a Roman eunuch."

"Eunuchs could grow beards?"

"Good point."

From time to time faces peered in from the sidewalk.

"It's so odd having you here. It's like — " But she got out of the car without finishing. It's like a high school reunion, she had been about to say.

She bought more date squares at the bakery: because they had been good, but also because it seemed right that what they had eaten, Jakob should share. "You think he would like these?"

"I don't know. What do people eat in Russia?"

"Black bread? Caviar?"

At the liquor store Christopher insisted on getting the best wine they had, then wondered if Jakob would want vodka. "In fact," Melanie remembered, "there's a Polish brandy that some of the farmers around here drink." But when she asked, the clerk said it had been "delisted" because someone had found tiny

108

pieces of glass at the bottom of some bottles. "Not that the glass would hurt you," he added, "if you could take the other."

They were standing in line at the cash register, and it seemed that everyone was looking at her, smiling with peculiar significance. She wanted to run.

Finally they were in the car again. Now that she was getting used to the new Christopher, sinking into the 3-D face, the mumbly voice, the comfortable knocked-about feeling of him, it was enough just to be close, her arm and shoulder brushing against his every time she shifted gears or turned. Not at all like driving with David. David was the opposite of Christopher: contained, intense, elusive, a predator always ready to explode. Or at least he had been when she still wanted that. Now he was only contained, separate, an ageing mystery whose name, unwritten, always topped the list of the oppressed who must be cared for. Prisoner of the marital wars. Prisoner of pride. Prisoner of loyalty. Prisoner of the fact that although she didn't want him, she needed him.

"You don't have to be faithful to me," David had declared the week before they got married.

"But I want to."

"Today you want to. But I'm fifteen years older than you."

"Don't say that."

"One day I'll suddenly be old and you will still be young. So I'm telling you, Melanie, not to be discussed, that I release you unconditionally—whenever, for whatever reason—"

"I don't accept."

"You will," David had predicted. But she hadn't, aside from her single one-night aberration, an involuntary lapse she felt guilty about for years afterwards.

Even before David, when she terrified herself with her promiscuity, she hadn't wanted Christopher. The opposite. In that era before David, when men were her means of filling up the night, she had needed Christopher too much to use him up in one of those brief dramas of which every line was absolutely predictable. David, at first, was just another of these. And then she'd decided to test herself, to cut out meaningless sex the way others stopped smoking; only her excuse would be that she was waiting for a man she knew, an older man, a Canadian university professor who was in love with her and whom she was going to join as soon as they could both decide to make the commitment.

"So this is it—the rolling hills, the grazing animals, the contented children—everything seems so peaceful."

They were driving along the edge of a lake. Melanie pulled over. On the opposite shore was a string of cottages and in front of the cottages a motor launch was towing a bronzed waterskier. The wind was blowing away from them—all that could be heard from the motor was a low buzz, while the skier, wearing a white bathing suit and a deep tan, zigzagged in and out of her own wake, triumphantly throwing one arm in the air every time she leapt the crest.

"And you? Are you busy? Happy? Did you know you were in our papers a few months ago? There was something about the movie you're supposed to be making. I meant to send you the clipping."

She had found just the right voice for saying it. A casual voice with no loose edges. As though the book—or as David called it, "this sex-soaked piece of trash"—were permanently and totally forgotten.

"Do you mind?"

"Of course not. Who's going to play me? Someone sexy I hope. You always had a very romantic idea of me that way. I'd love to see it on the screen. Are you writing the script?"

She had shown the book to Levin. He had brought it back, called her "the Desert Sex Queen", made her laugh.

The boat motor suddenly cut out; the skier was floundering in the water, and the boat was circling slowly back towards her. Just as, Melanie thought, Christopher's career had begun to flounder after the success of *Ape Man*. Not that there was anything wrong with the book—but it was trespassing and he should have known better. Must have known better. If it was money he needed, surely he could have come to her—that was what David had said.

Before the book was published, when they were still the best of friends, Christopher had been her confidant. The one she would call at midnight to tell her troubles, her doubts to—the one she would phone because he was the only one, except for Bronski, whose voice could fill the night. She would call him late, when the rates were down. In London it would be six or seven in the morning but Christopher would be awake and working, his voice full of the energy of dawn and his marathon sessions at the typewriter, while she, staggering tired and afraid of her nightmares, listened to the latest of his absurd adventures. "But does it make you happy?" she always insisted on asking him and he would say she was the only woman in the world who cared for him enough to ask that question. "Send them to me," she would joke. "Send them to me and I'll teach them respect." But of course he never did. Whoever Christopher's women were, she'd never actually met one. Sometimes, before calling him, she would try to cheer herself up by reading one of his blood-and-thunder historical romances. Violent death, cosmic sex, preposterous historical machinations: when she was in analysis she had talked about Christopher's novels. She'd wanted her analyst to say he was writing them because he couldn't face his own life; instead he'd explained that Christopher could write such things because he didn't really believe them.

The skier was up again, the boat making new loops around the bay.

Melanie looked at her watch. It was two hours since they had set out for town. At Drancy they had passed whole days starting conversations, dropping them, sitting side by side and looking out at things for which they had no words. Then, another day, another week, taking up where they had left off. Even now, she supposed, it would be easy to look at the lake until the sun went down, then drive back to the farmhouse, still without talking, and rejoin the others. Only Bronski would have understood what they had been doing, would be able to join into their secret language, which was silence.

She turned her eyes back to Christopher. He was smiling at her, a slow comfortable smile that demanded no response. At Drancy she would watch his face for whole evenings, ride the hours out on the slowly darkening contours of his cheek, the twitch of his mouth as he read a book Bronski had managed to find for him.

She closed the door, started the motor.

When they got back to the house the others were sitting in lawn chairs in the shade. As the car drew up they turned towards it like an audience at a play waiting to discover what entertainment the next scene might bring. But by the time she had actually carried the shopping bags up to the house the others were talking among themselves, ignoring her; except for Bronski, whose eyes followed her as she passed.

She meant to go to Jakob when the groceries were put away, but by that time Benjamin had joined her and she was telling him about Levin, clearing the table, doing dishes, starting to prepare for the next meal as soon as the kitchen was clean—all of these operations interrupted by the telephone ringing.

While she was on the phone Bronski walked by her, on his way upstairs; it was her turn to observe—his to be caught—a sweet old man with the body of a giant. His face turned furtively from hers as he passed, too shy to express whatever it was he must feel going off to sleep in his new bed, his new home. And seeing him like this, a child with his face averted, Melanie felt a sudden rush of maternal tenderness and had to hold herself back from hurrying over to help him to his room, tuck him in, whisper that from now on he had a *home*.

By the time more phone calls had been attended to, the final letters of the day written, the dining-room table set and the dinner begun, it was almost sundown. Leaving Helen to finish, Melanie went upstairs. Just as she had promised Levin, she took her final pill of the day. Then she changed into her bathing suit and walked down to the dock.

All afternoon the sky had been a clear and brilliant blue. Now, as the sun hovered above the trees across the lake, ribs of cloud curved around the horizon and arced towards the dock where Melanie was sitting, feet dangling in the water. A few years after she had got back to the United States there had been a summer that she had spent in northern New York with a university classmate. Wealthy summer estates surrounded the lake; the motor launches had been the fanciest and the most powerful money could buy; there was even, for the children of the wealthy, a young and muscular coach hired to teach them how to perform tricks on the fiberglass skis their parents bought from air-conditioned sports stores.

Every morning her friend visited a house where another kind of teacher lived—a young rabbi who was giving religious instruction to three young ladies on the lake who were to be married. Melanie—house guest, fellow Jew, survivor of Drancy—had gone with her girlfriend. Elaine Bachmann had been her name. Melanie at twenty was still thin, underdeveloped and without marital prospects. Her hair, long and thickly braided, used to bounce from her shoulders that summer: after swimming she would take off the elastics and wring her hair dry. "Your dog tails are dripping," Elaine would say to her. Because pig tails wouldn't have been kosher. Because Melanie, after swimming, would shake her head like a dog shaking itself dry. Because the young rabbi—so claimed Elaine and the other two girls though Melanie denied it—looked at Melanie with solemn doggy eyes as he begged her to explain how she, of all people, after what she had seen and experienced, could fail to take seriously her religious duties as a Jewess.

Melanie, sitting on the dock, looked down at the way her thighs spread against the weathered cedar. That other summer her thighs had been tanned and narrow; it was her friend's mother who had the white spreading thighs, the folds across the belly, the fringe of black hairs along her upper lip. Elaine's mother, too, who had told Melanie she had better be careful or she would grow up to be "a selfish bitch, just like your mother, if you'll excuse my saying so—but you must have asked yourself how you ended up where you did."

Melanie unwrapped the bandage from her finger, dipped her hand into the water. The cut made by the razor that morning was now just a tiny pink nick. Amazing how quickly the pendulum could swing. Her pendulum. Just thinking about how peaceful she felt was enough to start her fluttering.

Out on the water two loons swam in slow circles. Melanie slid the towel from her shoulders, climbed carefully down the ladder until she was waist-deep in the water, then pushed out. Floating on her back she could see the long barred clouds crystallizing with the deepening light. Ever since she had discovered Bronski was still alive she had wanted to believe she could retrieve him, bring him to her, restore him to life so that he might do the same for her. Now she had a nervous feeling in her belly, of danger, as though Bronski were an infant and she had been a bad mother to leave him unattended.

## 4. *Old Numbers Never Die*

He had slept, if you could call that dream sleeping. If you could call dreaming that dive into Dr. Lydia's cupboard. "Comrades." Dr. Lydia's face above theirs. Red-veined eyes. The stink of her breath that filled the cupboard even when she was outside, standing guard, while he and Anna sweated to fill it with their own odours, their own ocean of juices. "Happy birthday, comrades." Dr. Lydia's face swimming into the candlelight. Cheekbones swollen and deformed, thick hide-like skin lumped over them, monster eyes. Then she withdrew, locking the door on him and Anna, the one whole night they would ever have together. Six hours behind a locked door. To plunge and plunge again. To suck and bite and swallow and croon and promise and lie. Six hours behind a locked door in a suburban Moscow hospital for model mental patients. Six hours for the future to become past. Dr. Lydia's lopsided limp as she patrolled the hall. Her hoarse voice whispering into the keyhole. "Comrades, I trust you're not giving each other diseases for which the state must provide the cure. Comrades, do you have to piss? Remember, your lovenest is my bed. And I joined the Party for free love, comrades, please be reminded that alternate fucks are to be donated to the people."

He had woken, his head full of Dr. Lydia's breath and the silky feel of Anna's back, his chest slick with perspiration. His shirt came off like a bandage, leaving his skin feeling new, cool, raw to the small breeze that was rustling through the leaves and throwing small jets of cold air through the screened window. He lit a cigarette. For a moment, sticky with drying sweat, hot and shivering at the same time, he could have been back at the hospital, the dormitory, staggering out of bed after days of needle-induced torpor.

He crossed the hall to the bathroom and splashed water on his face. Through the window poured the soft smells of late afternoon. From his room he got his shoes, then he went downstairs and outside. Another cigarette. When he dreamed of the cupboard the air was always thick and yellow, a sour fog of fear and remorse. He walked over to examine the barbecue machine David had shown him earlier in the day. On the table beside it, enclosed in a large glass casserole, slabs of steak were marinating in a dark sauce. He lifted the lid, poked in a finger, licked it. A winy pungent taste filled his mouth.

He reached out and touched the gun-metal grey hood of the barbecue. It made a fragile ping when he snapped a fingernail against it. Ping. Ping.

The gas canister was large enough to be an oxygen tank. Jakob found himself examining the smooth pastel-blue paint job, the carefully machined parts joining canister to tube, tube to stippled grill with its permanently installed lumps of imitation charcoal.

In this late afternoon light, the colours were rich and liquid. Plonked awkwardly into the thick grass, his shoes—stained, scraped, blotched by rain and oil, crinkled and ridged like abandoned skins—looked as intrusive and out of place as they had on Rabbi Goldman's carpet. How perfect it would be to simply float right out of that uncomfortable lumpy leather, float away from everything old and broken in his life and drift through this strange paradise. Become an insect burrowing into the lush grass. A dragonfly darting through the changing light. One of the birds chattering on the wires that connected house and barns, flying from tree to tree, from one leaf-shadowed hideout to the next.

At the hospital he had for several summers been the gardener. But despite his best efforts the flowers were always eaten by birds and insects, and there was never seed or water enough to make the patchy grass into the thick lawn requested by the director. Finally one year he did make the grass grow. But the planned construction of a new wing brought trucks carrying concrete blocks to gouge their way across his grass during a week of incessant rain. When the rain stopped the building didn't begin. For three years the building of the new wing did not begin. Then one day the trucks returned and the blocks were carted away.

The removal of the blocks was an improvement: more ground was available for landscaping; the prospective noise and mess of construction had been blown away like an unwelcome cloud. Moreover, it had become clear that the piles of concrete blocks posed other menaces. Change. The possibility of becoming too important, of attracting outside investigations.

Bronski looked around him. The house and barns were nestled into the tiny hills above the lake. Overhead the evening sky was filled with the colours of blood and of war, of the earth torn open, of the violence of life. But against this thundering light the trees loomed like massive shadows of goodness, glowing like the faces of his hosts, with the fullness of their love, their desire to dissolve earthly cares in their rich embrace.

When Melanie had written about a retreat in the country he had imagined a primitive boarded cabin in the midst of a woods. And yet, according to David, even this was not a place for the very rich—although he had promised to show him such places. This was a farm so poor, David said, that its previous owners had virtually abandoned it in order to find work in the city.

He walked through the gate to the grassy area between house and barns. One summer when he was a boy his mother had taken him to visit an uncle's farm outside Warsaw. This uncle, it turned out, was related to the famous Marie Curie. They were to travel by cart with a neighbouring farmer who brought vegetables to the Jewish market in Warsaw and would have empty space on the return trip. They had met the neighbour at the market, then spent from noon until nightfall bouncing first through the city of Warsaw, then into the increasingly wild countryside.

He had never been beyond their small neighbourhood; everything he saw struck him with fear, wonder, bewilderment. They arrived after sunset. Their relatives had already lit the candles and, as it was Sabbath, were saying the prayers. The city visitors were greeted, their suitcases put in the corner of the house, then the prayers were finished and the evening meal begun. When it was time to go to sleep, Jakob discovered he would be spending the night on a small wooden platform set on stones above a dirt floor. All night his sleep was interrupted by the sound of strange insects, the movement of animals outside the house, odours he had never smelled, sighs from the mouths of strangers. In the morning he went outside and saw that their house was part of a small village. Between the cracks of the house hung bits of rag meant to keep out the winter cold, and over the one real glass window was a curtain said to have come from the Holy Land. Adjoining his own room was a shed with two cows and an ox: these animals had been the source of the heavy breathing for which he had spent half the night inventing explanations.

At the mental hospital there had also been a barn. A large one—also at times a good place for heavy breathing—stocked with animals that were supposed to provide meat, therapy and currency for the inmates. During the lectures on collective effort—delivered during a certain period by a Dr. Gordunov, whose strange but enthusiastic gestures were taken by the inmates as an unconscious declaration of those very homosexual tendencies he often denounced—love of animals, love for the soil of the motherland, heroic struggle for the welfare of the people, were all recommended with great enthusiasm.

Jakob opened the gate, walked around to the front. Inside the barn was dark; the long centre aisle David had cleaned that morning shone like an expectant runway.

Beside one of the stalls lay a bale of hay. Jakob sat down on it, scraped his shoes against the cement, lit a new cigarette. Flies were beginning to buzz around him; at the door of the barn he could see swallows swooping in and out of the framed light.

"Put out to pasture." The first time he had encountered that phrase, part of one of those jokes Western scientists loved to use to preface their papers, he had spent days puzzling over its meaning. According to the paper, So-and-so's theory should have been "put out to pasture"— Now, sitting in the barn, he realized he was being put out to pasture: meaning that he no longer deserved the shelter of the barn? That free grass rather than expensive oats now constituted his proper diet? That he could spend his days chewing grass rather than in harness? All at once, of course: the essence of translation was to preserve all the inner contradictions. As with his translation from Moscow to Canada. To this farm, for example, a perfect ambiguous mix of the peasant village where, a few years after the summer visit, his uncle had been shot by a passing soldier whose crime went untried because he claimed the bullet had been intended for a wild dog, and the mental home where overdoses of love and pain had finally sealed his heart from both past and future.

He had spread his hands on his knees and was rubbing his palms back and forth, his whole body swaying as he scratched them against his pants. The night after Anna's death he had rocked this way, back and forth, scratching at his palms until by morning the skin was rubbed raw. From his right hand one finger was entirely missing, from his left, two and a half. These absences had been accomplished with an axe, as a punishment for stealing food. A few weeks after the incident with his hands, he had been given identity papers—his first in a decade—and allowed to leave the refugee camp to work in a restricted area. Aside from these absences were certain other fundamental gaps: a wife he had loved—but whose marriage to him had caused her to be killed; an infant daughter he had tried to save by abandoning her to the protection of another man; Anna.

119

His wife, Gabrielle, had been innocent, demure, petite. His daughter, an infant of whom he had just a few memories—but not of the last time he had held her, the last time he had kissed her, the last time he had looked into her eyes—had been reduced in his mind to pure speculation and a promise to God that because he had deserted her, he must never seek her out. The worst gap was Anna. Perhaps because he had met her after he thought he had given up all hope. Perhaps because being older, more vulnerable, less whole, he had needed her more. Gabrielle he had loved as a young man who still believes in himself loves a young and pretty woman. With Anna he had abandoned everything—as at death everything is abandoned. Or perhaps he had simply given her his soul because only she had wanted it. Anna had been the worst loss; and also the last loss, because after her no further attachment would be possible.

He was rocking back and forth, grinding his palms against the shiny knees of the pants he had brought for starting his new life. So, this was it. The new life. And on the first afternoon of the new life he was reviewing a few of the high and low points of the old, while sitting in the barn of his benefactors, looking at the blurred milk-and-honey blue sky that hung above the grass—the pasture he was finally being put out to.

He stood up. The light from the barn door was too bright to face. He turned around and walked deeper into the barn. At the end of the stalls was a door. He pushed it open, found himself in a small concrete room with cobwebbed windows.

Against one wall was a desk covered in straw dust. In front of it was a swivel armchair. He pulled it out, sat down, lit himself a new cigarette, careful to spit on the head of the dead match for safety.

Through the filthy window could be seen the house. And there was, he now noticed, a separate door leading from the office. When Melanie had started writing him she had talked proudly about their farm, their beef cattle, the tears she cried every time calves were sold.

One of the desk drawers was partly open. He pulled it farther: nothing but a deserted mouse nest. Then he tried the other. It held several square cardboard packages. He picked one of them up. It was covered with dust, heavy. But even as he pushed the dust away he realized it was filled with cartridges.

The rifle was in a pine cupboard that looked as though it had been knocked together a century ago. He cleaned one of the cartridges on his shirt-tail, then fitted it into the rifle. After Anna's death he had prayed to come across such a weapon. After Anna's death he had been overwhelmed by the desire for revenge, the desire to inflict pain, the desire to hear in other throats the echo of his own pain. Balancing the rifle in his hands, he walked into the empty barn and shot the bullet into a bale of hay. There was a report, not too loud. He went back into the office, started a new cigarette, smoked it while he cleaned the rest of the cartridges. Then he returned them to the dusty box, put the box and the rifle in their places.

When he stood up a wave of dizziness gripped him. A strange thought arrived. Perhaps life was being wrapped in such dizziness, cocoons of confusion—and death a butterfly flying free.

He was walking now, out into the brightness beyond the barn. He kept going until he had crested one of the hills and could look down at the whole valley—fields stretching out towards the neighbouring farm, dots of cattle grazing; and then, turning back to the house, he could see the farm buildings protected by broad leafy trees, cars parked in the driveway, an oval of lake surrounded by green, the single road winding its leisurely way through the details of this gentle iron exile.

## 5. Useful Tricks with Counting

"Bitch," Melanie said. "I told you never to stand in front of mirrors." But there she was, facing the heart-shaped mirror framed in cherrywood that David had bought her after they moved to the farm. How perfect that when she looked into the heart David had given her she would get nothing of David, only her own uncertain self. "Go downstairs," Melanie said. Downstairs they were drinking, laughing, eating the little snacks she and Helen had arranged in perfect circles on their best plates.

At Drancy it was Christopher who found out what happened to those taken on the trains. Jakob was the comforter but Christopher was the spy, trading information the way others traded food or books. Thin, elusive, everybody's friend, he would disappear for hours at a time, even overnight. Then in the middle of the night, or while she was sitting lost in a corner of the courtyard, Melanie would discover him by her side again, silently watching. When the rations were to be reduced, a new roundup to arrive, increased quotas for the trains to be announced, Christopher was always the first to know. But she didn't believe his stories about the death camps. A few weeks later, photographs were smuggled in. One showed a pile of bodies with a bulldozer poised to shove them into a ditch. All she could wish was that she wouldn't be the one with the leg sticking out to one side: a naked exposed skeletal leg protruding from the safety of the general mass like a stick from a bird's nest.

"We were melted down anyway," she said to Levin once. "Just thinking about it melted me down."

She had Levin's coin between her knuckles, was tracing it along her cheekbones, her jaw, the ridge of her nose. Suicide by skinning. To be found a perfect skeleton, eyes and teeth in place, everything else piled neatly beside.

She had read an article about buzzards. "They eat the eyes first," the writer had explained, "because in the eye is the hard condensed essence of the soul."

A good girl, she had taken her evening medicine. Or forgotten. Had she forgotten? In front of the mirror was her glass of water, her vial of pills. She was certain, almost certain, she could remember looking in the mirror and sticking out her tongue. A long red road. In the middle of the road she had placed the pill. Pink and shiny with a crease down the centre. "Cunt," she had said. She could distinctly remember saying the word. "Cunt," she had said, the way she would say it at Stalag Estomac. There the word sounded harmless, ridiculous, comic. In her own room it made an ugly vibration. "First Commandment: thou shalt not say cunt in thine own bedroom."

The door opened, Timmy appeared.

"I was practising magic," Melanie said.

She approached Timmy, the coin still between her knuckles.

Timmy stood, frozen.

"You see this coin?"

Timmy nodded.

She reached out.

"It's time for supper," Timmy said.

"Count to three."

She put her hand behind her back. "I bet you can't find my quarter." Timmy reached around her. She had it buried in her fist and as he tried to pry it open she began to tickle him. Timmy shrieked with laughter. They fell down onto the carpet, Timmy still laughing as he worked on her fingers, Melanie digging her free hand into his hard ribs as he squirmed.

Finally he rolled away, the coin in his hand; then, waving it in front of him, ran down the stairs.

"Creep," she yelled after him. But her blood was settled. Without looking in the mirror she pushed her hair back in place, then crossed the hall to David's room, where the telephone was.

Levin answered on the first ring.

"Timmy stole your magic quarter. I wish you were here."

"You okay?"

"Okay now."

"Good."

"I still can't do mirrors."

"Where are you?"

"David's room. It's like a monk's cell in here. I wonder where he hides his dirty magazines." Levin laughed. "It's not funny. Levin, for God's sake, how am I going to get through this?" There was a silence at the other end of the telephone but Melanie knew his answer, which was that she would get through this— or anything else—a second at a time, that whether she was skinning herself alive, peeling tomatoes or tickling Timmy, her life was going to roll by a second at a time, a slow flawed unstoppable train. Over the telephone wires came a light hiss. Until a few years ago David had insisted on saving money by having a party line, which meant that she could imagine her desperation phone calls being overheard by a whole string of neighbours. The way she had listened to Florence MacFarlane the day she broke down sobbing while telling her own mother that the bank had foreclosed. The neighbours had hung up one by one, lightening the line, except for Melanie, who *had* to listen, and Brian Thomas's mother, who had finally interrupted to say she was driving right over with a bottle of rye and they would drown the fucking bastards.

She went down to the dining room thinking that at least her eyes weren't red. Though it wouldn't have mattered because the lights were off. Just a few candles in the silver holders: another auction, another pain-stained gift from David.

She sat down in the empty chair between Christopher and Jakob. "To our Queen," Christopher said, raising his glass, and across the table David raised his, bent towards her, dipping his head in mock reverence, then coming up, and for a moment there was a little chink in his face and she felt a beat of that current, that true strong current that had drawn her to him. "My King," she almost replied, would have thirty years ago, but now didn't have time to get it out because before she could even begin his face had gone cold and impassive again. Tricky David, yes, he knew how to cut her off, how to slide from lover to enemy. There had been a guard like that at Drancy: young, friendly, tense, and then one day when he noticed how she spent all her time with Christopher he had turned cold as metal, hounded the two of them until finally he had found an excuse to jump Christopher, bury his boot in Christopher's mouth.

The bones of her fingers were clicking noisily against each other. She pressed her hands together to calm then, then carefully reached for her glass and took a big swallow of wine. "To my men," she announced. "If I was Napoleon we could conquer the world." She drank again. The wine was smooth and settling. She held out her glass to Christopher, who refilled it. Timmy was staring at her from the end of the table. "Thief," Melanie growled and Timmy smirked.

In front of Jakob were his cigarettes. Melanie took one. Half rose and leaned into a candle to light it. The heat rubbed like a cat against her face.

She inhaled. Then looked down. There was a plate in front of her: roast beef, pickled beets, broccoli, boiled new potatoes she herself had scrubbed and readied for the pot. "Food," a voice rumbled. Jakob was turned towards her, and now his arm settled heavily over her shoulders. Its weight pulled her down into her chair, dissolved the room into a warm mellow haze. At the other end of the table voices melted comfortably together, "Food," Jakob rumbled again. He took the cigarette from her hand. Melanie leaned into his chest. Jakob's hand was on her head, stroking her hair, her neck, as though she were a child, the way he had when she was a child. "No white sauce," Jakob rumbled. "Herr Hitler guarantees this is the most racially pure food in all of Paris." He had grown but so had she. So it was perfect again — to be leaning into his chest, warm and sheltered in his cave, listening peacefully to the rumble of his voice as their trains moved through the night and she ate.

"You know what I admire about you, Christopher?"

"No." Or perhaps he had only nodded. Being, as it were, a guest at the house of the tight-assed little snot Melanie had married.

"You put that whole experience behind you."

They had been sitting outside, beside David's grill, having a drink of the duty-free scotch Christopher had brought for exactly this purpose—a little long-delayed fence mending. Not that the fence would survive the *Ape Man* movie, if it was ever made. And what would the host think if he knew that in Christopher's luggage was a copy of the script he was revising?

"Put it behind me?"

"Exactly. No tragic aura. No black pit of depression. No compulsive returning to the past."

Now Christopher, at the dinner table between David and Melanie, was aware of David talking to him again. A smooth voice this professor had, one used to hearing itself speak uninterrupted. "I read his poetry," David was saying. "A remarkable man."

Christopher leaned towards him, because David was speaking softly in order to avoid being overheard, and then he caught Melanie looking at him, winking. At Drancy, when she came across him talking to someone else, Melanie would wink at him this way: *we've still got our secret*. But perhaps David was right and he didn't have it any more. Had long ago amputated it, along with whatever part of himself should have forgotten Melanie, married, done whatever it was normal people do. *Child of the Camps* he could have written, a searing little memoir of a

126

childhood spent in the midst of death. And then moved on. Instead of cutting it off—whenever or however he'd done it—then coming back to Paris where he could hover at the scene of the crime, at the grave of his amputated self. "What do you think he'll do here?" David was asking. Someone had put on music so now they seemed to be in a room of their own defined by noise and candlelight.

And then without waiting for an answer David reached for the bottle, emptied it into their glasses.

"Cheers," Christopher said, raised his glass to clink with David's. The wine tasted sour and thin.

"I'll get another bottle," David said.

"Let me." And before his host could reply, Christopher was on his feet, had gone out the door of the dining room and made his way to the kitchen pantry, where he'd put the wine bought in town that afternoon.

"Christopher," came Melanie's voice. Clear. Assured. "We need." At the airport she had been the uncertain one. Flushed, nervous, ready to fall apart. So unsure of herself: face constantly changing, retreating, calling for help. But after she had almost knocked that poor girl into the ditch she had taken hold.

The corkscrew was waiting beside the two bottles. But wine, of which he had already drunk much this evening, no longer interested him. Whisky did.

At this moment he was on his third official whisky—official whisky being that drunk from the glass and mixed with ice and water in order not to taste too tempting. Someone else must also have been feeling the need, since the forty-ounce bottle of Glenlivet he had bought at the Paris airport and not opened until a few hours ago was now almost half empty. David, no doubt. The little man had a big thirst. In his honour, Christopher decided, he would add a new scene to the movie. A scene in which he explained to the Canadian professor his incredible luck in landing Melanie.

"There is something lush, sensuous, overripe about her face," he would start. Just to make him nervous. Then, to torture him further, he would suggest that while the face—with its quick changes, its textures, its dazzling ability to portray moods and feelings—compelled, the body appeared innocent of sex. The corruption of sex, to be exact; or to be more exact, the corruption which desire too often fulfilled leaves upon a woman's body.

Christopher reminded himself that critics, especially female critics, lay in wait for such thoughts about women. Outdated, they would scream. Male presumption. Why should sex corrupt women while it makes men mature? Are women to be denied while men romp with impunity?

From the dining room came the sounds of the others. They were happy but he was not. He sipped at the drink he had manufactured. He lifted it high, regarded the somewhat cloudy liquid by the light of the bare bulb that hung from the pantry ceiling, poured it down the sink. When his glass was empty he rinsed it, dried it with a towel providentially at hand. Then he filled it with Glenlivet undiluted. Tonight he would take his single malt uncompromised, untainted by ice made from the water of a foreign country. Eventually he would fall to sleep drunk, ashamed, yet proud of his meaningless idiocy. And in the morning he would make his reservation to fly back to Paris.

He emptied his glass again, this time not into the sink, and poured another. "Christopher Lewis, you sewer," he said to himself.

"Christopher." Melanie's voice peremptory now, full of itself.

"*J'arrive*," Christopher shouted back.

"*Il arrive*," Melanie echoed obscenely and the others burst into new laughter.

In front of him were the two bottles of wine. Someone, perhaps himself, had removed their corks. Taking one bottle in each hand he set forth.

When he arrived back in the dining room, the sputtering candlelight had drawn all the faces together, as though they were in the midst of a seance. Melanie turned to Christopher—*dazzling ability to portray moods and feelings*—and a certain part of Christopher's brain advanced the hypothesis that he had left this room apparently totally sober, so sober that no question of his sobriety could even have occurred—and had now returned visibly drunk. Another part of his brain recorded the fact that while he set down the first bottle, the second tipped slightly, and released an insignificant stream of liquid that was now making its way down his wrist.

He mumbled something about forgetting his glass, then backed away—out of the light, out of the room, down the hall towards the pantry. The voices behind him mixed together as the old sods cackled and cried their way into the night. "A grave crisis of international proportions has gripped a usually sleepy rural corner of the Dominion of Canada," he intoned to no one. "Swamped by an unprecedented wave of emotion from an old friend, visiting British cultural diplomat Christopher Lewis found it necessary to declare an unprecedented emergency and, in order to save the dignity of Empire, perform an auto-transfusion."

He extended his arm to hold the bottle to the light. Fingerprints indeed. One of the moths that had been circling the bulb landed on his forearm. Whitish-grey, soft textured wings, long hooked legs that tangled now in the hairs of his arm as the wings fluttered in a panic. Christopher brought the moth closer to his eyes. Now he could see the creature's fear, its strange face-like configuration of antennae and hairs twisting with the effort to be free. "In the morning you'll be dead," Christopher reminded it. It didn't seem to care. Christopher shook his arm so the moth could fly away. "Visiting diplomat sets loose imprisoned native," he announced. He turned on the tap, let the water run through his palms for a moment. He dug his knuckles into the corners of his eyes, pushed his wet hands over his scalp and through his hair.

The voices in the other room had escalated. Christopher poured the rest of the Glenlivet into his waiting glass. This way, at least, he would be removing temptation from the mouth of the anonymous thief. On the other hand, even the absence of temptation, like temptation itself, was nothing more than an illusion; in fact Christopher had knowledge of a second bottle of Glenlivet strategically hidden in the bizarre converted barn-loft to which David had so proudly shown him.

In the kitchen window, blackened by the night, Christopher saw himself reflected. Baggy pants, bulging waist, wide shoulders. Silvery hair and matching white shirt open against the heat.

Christopher sipped at his whisky. He realized he was on the verge of a new novel, his first in years. It would be about his best subject, Melanie, and would begin with the author drinking while offstage rang the silvery laugh of Melanie herself. *There is something lush, sensuous, overripe about her face*, he would start. But that sounded like an advertisement for a particularly desirable mango. Indeed, why not *her skin had the soft texture of a ripe mango*. On the other hand, Shakespeare never started with his main character. Or with a metaphor about tropical fruit. Why should Christopher Lewis fall into the trap William Shakespeare had so cleverly avoided? Christopher Lewis would begin his *magnum opus* with something completely absent from the plays of William Shakespeare. He would open with the taste of scotch whisky bruised by Canadian ice. He would begin with the fact that for reasons unknown to himself he was not, at the moment, prepared to be in the same room as Melanie Lansing Winters. He would start by opening the second bottle of Glenlivet because the first had been merely a crutch with which to begin the slow walk through the foothills leading to the true mountain, the mountain whose size and shape he was beginning to sense in the darkness outside. And then, without exactly knowing how it happened, he *was* outside, in the darkness, moving away from the house and across the lawn towards the dark plateau overlooking the lake.

On his knees, in the grass, face down to the ground. Not sick, only spinning. He waved his head back and forth, grooming his cheeks against the cool dark blades.

There was a breeze. Leaves whispered, rubbed themselves together. Above, the sky: dark blue, electric with the silver light of a crescent moon. Beyond the noise of the leaves, the high-pitched stutters cheeps whines of insects, came a loud shriek. He jerked upright. Again the shriek, this time a duet that started, stopped, interrupted itself with mournful solos climaxed by savage yowling. Raccoons, porcupines, anonymous furry things with their throats opened to the night. Either trying to kill each other or reproducing, if there was a difference.

He lit a cigarette. From the edge of the lawn he could survey the house, the barns, the darkly sculpted horizon. He had gone into the darkness, ready to scale the mountain he sensed there, but now the mountain was nowhere to be seen.

There was a sharp, crawling sensation on his chin. He jerked forward to slap, the back of his shirt split open, and he felt a sudden stripe of cool wind form itself on his back. The noises started again: Christopher found himself considering those throats, those mouths, those teeth. Chests pumping, bellies in spasms, throats ululating to a climax — Bronski would feel close to those animals, Bronski who had spent a whole lifetime crying silently into the darkness.

And himself? Had he spent his life crying—silently or otherwise—into the darkness?

From the house came the sound of a door slamming. Melanie's voice calling his name. He stepped back into the shadows.

But like the mountain, the place to which he had retreated didn't exist. Beneath his foot, nothing—a drop. He fell hard, his ankle twisting first, then his whole body contorting as he began to bounce down the steep slope, every bump accompanied by twigs and roots jabbing into his belly, cutting at his neck and face.

He landed on the beach, beside the stairway cut into the hill. Wading into the lake he splashed water on his face and neck, cleaned out his mouth. Would this also be part of the novel? Or perhaps he should be writing not a novel but the script for one of those modern films, a French film in which the *auteur* becomes the main character.

He had a picture of himself on the screen—arms extended, bottle waving triumphantly in the night air, bare bleeding chest exposed to the summery breezes, when something inside his stomach gave way. His intestines convulsed, his mouth twisted open to expel a thick stream tasting of whisky and blood.

By the time he had made his way back to the house they were playing music. Through the open windows, weaving among the lilac bushes, the trees, the imperfect blackness of the night, came the slow sentimental strains of a Schubert concerto. When he finally got to the window he saw that Melanie had taken Jakob in her arms. Formally, solemnly, gliding ever so slowly from one precarious step to the next, they were waltzing in and out of the candlelight.

## 6. *Infinity Minus One*

There was a presence in the room. David sat up. He put his hand to his chest. His heart was beating, as always—as almost always—strong and steady. Death, yes, he had been dreaming about Death, dreaming that Death, in the shape of Jakob Bronski, had become a guest in his household, that hidden in the scarred flesh of Jakob Bronski's hands was the weapon that would kill him.

He had never thought of Death this way before. Death as a person, a presence, a force. The first time he had visited the remains of the Canadian trenches of the Great War, he had dreamed, every night for weeks, of open graves full of soldiers. Soldiers who had died intact. Soldiers who had died of disease. Soldiers whose bodies had been torn apart by the engines of war. What had been so terrible in those dreams had been the *sounds* of the dying; an inhuman music that had risen above the trenches in what, David had informed his young man's diary, was the inhuman music of time.

He tried to sit up. Or at least he thought of sitting up. Then he looked around his bedroom—the separate bedroom he had moved into after the stroke so that Melanie wouldn't be constantly awakened by his insomnia. "I don't want to die,"

David Winters said to himself. Professor Doctor David Winters. His mouth opened, out came the words with a forced raspy sound. "I don't want to die," he said again.

There had been the stroke. Also, before and since, other incidents. Not that he was prematurely old. The opposite. Especially when he was in his sixties, people had always looked shocked when he told them his age.

He looked at his watch. He could wake Melanie. Explain that Death was stalking him, that even though he had laughed with her and her friends all evening, danced until midnight, drunk wine and brandy and carried on a conversation about modern films and psycho-politics, in fact he had spent the whole evening worrying about dying. Had kept imagining himself as a skeleton, Christopher as a skeleton, Benjamin and Helen and Timmy as skeletons. That he had been afraid he would fall down the stairs when he went to the bathroom, that he would lose control of his legs while dancing, that he would wake up in some unimaginable beyond when he lay down in his bed and went to sleep.

He switched on the light. This was his bedroom. This was fear. This was the primal reaction of the overgenerous host who has wined and dined his worst enemies. The curtains were flapping in the open window. No doubt they had caused his nightmares. He hated flapping curtains, open windows.

He realized that he was looking at the ceiling again. Since his stroke he had spent, while the world slept, thousands of hours staring upwards. This particular ceiling was one he himself had painted. When he bought the house it had been a flamboyant pink. Now it was a sandy off-white, an uneven, rolling desert with dunes, lacunae, places where the colour was mounded and others where the original pink showed through.

In the desert was where he had met Melanie. Even then, he had already felt old. Needing something to clear him out, as he had said to the woman he was engaged to, his "fiancée" who had so believed in their coming marriage that she had picked out a pattern for their knives and forks. So believed in their marriage that when he told her about Melanie she had exploded with rage. "Do you have to go to bed with every woman who makes a grab for your dick?"

"She did not, as you so crudely put it, 'make a grab for my dick'."

"Don't apologize, my dear man, correct me. Let me set the record straight. *Melanie did not make a grab for the professor's dick.* There. No, pray tell, what did happen? I mean, something must have happened. You said you slept together. Or did you mean that you both just lapsed into a coma at the same time? Or maybe before you even touched each other the earth moved, knocked you off your feet, and as you fell on top of her, quite accidentally, your fly unzipped and you pranged her."

In fact he had been sleeping by himself in the kitchen tent because he had been writing late and the simplest thing to do was to sleep in the tent with the table. At some point, after he had put out his lantern and crawled into his sleeping bag on the camp cot, the flap of the tent had opened. He had leapt up, startled; it was only Melanie, not knowing he was there, looking for privacy. She was frightened, she said. Nightmares. He knew nothing about her childhood then, only that she was an American graduate student, a friend of Christopher Lewis, the young British museum worker who had organized the expedition. She sat at the table. His cot was beside it, close enough to touch. He asked her what she was dreaming about but she wouldn't say. She seemed typical of a certain kind of university student—rich, spoiled, aimless. Eventually the conversation either stopped or became too boring to keep him awake. When he woke up again the night was deeper, blacker. Melanie was still sitting beside him in the wooden folding chair. She was holding his hand and talking to herself. It took him a few seconds to realize she was speaking not English but French. And then he understood that she wasn't speaking at all, not real words, she was merely counting to herself. From one to a thousand and back again. Simple counting, adding or subtracting one at a time, as though every number was a life given or a life taken away.

He lay without moving; listening to her whispers in the dry air.

Her hand gripped his tightly. Her mouth was open and her long hair masked her cheeks as she rocked back and forth. Slowly he had begun stroking her. Fingers. Hand. Forearm.

He moved to put his arm around her, then she slid over from her chair onto his cot, wound up like a snail on top of him, lying between his arms and the sleeping bag. That was the way she fell asleep, coiled. He could still remember the weight of her. In the morning she was gone but Christopher was in the tent, theatrically tiptoeing about as he prepared breakfast.

She had put a spell on him. That was the first thought that came: how else could he have simply fallen asleep, after weeks of celibacy, with a beautiful woman—even one who panted like an animal and counted to herself in French—in his arms? Now, David could feel her weight on him again, as though the spell were still unbroken. Although at the time he had decided the spell had been cast not by Melanie but by the desert, pressing them together, man and woman—the incomplete halves who could never join. Although the next night they did their best. Writhing on top of her in the pitch blackness of the kitchen tent, David had seen not Melanie's face but the open pit they had been working on that afternoon, the layered sand that protected, like thick peelings of time, its indecipherable nuggets of bone and rock.

"You mean you had a mystic experience fucking a graduate student."

Outside, away from the tents and the others, wearing thick sweaters and wrapped in a blanket, was where she had told him about Drancy. About Jakob Bronski, the unofficial camp medic to whom she had been sent the first time she got sick. Who made her his assistant and gave her a spiral notebook into which he would dictate things she was supposed to write down. Weights, heights, the shrinking numbers. Jakob Bronski, the giant who wasn't a doctor but seemed to believe that the illnesses might be cured simply by recording the symptoms, witnessing them, taking them away from the victim and putting them into his record books.

The desert sky. The soft insides of Melanie's thighs. The truth was that they had never truly decided. Not the clean decision they needed, the razor through time dividing before from after. Instead there had been a certain number of empty months, hour-long phone calls, letters thick with longing. Seized by this longing, he finally invited Melanie to visit him in Toronto. And there the seed was planted: Benjamin.

Melanie pregnant: instant marriage and then, instantly after, it seemed, the erotic and mournful surface of the beautiful student cracked and out came a desperate and driven woman with no idea who she was, how she wanted to live, how she was going to survive the terrifying prospect of giving birth.

"Lover" was the word Melanie used to use to describe her various men. Not Christopher. Although she never volunteered information about her affairs, she also refused to lie about them; and about Christopher she was always adamant—"I would never have gone to bed with him"—despite the fact that she routinely denounced the idea of marital fidelity as "the fascism of emotional laziness". Before they were married, that is. Before he found himself sliding from one affair to another with a strange ease he could never have predicted—chain-screwing his way through graduate school, secretaries, conferences, trips abroad. Why me? David would ask himself—no stud, no looker, no spender, just a modest good-natured lover of life without clothes.

He dressed. He closed the window. It was the middle of the night. Imagine that: an old man awake in the middle of the night, going over ancient romances and disappointments.

He put on his slippers, opened his door. Up and down the dark hall, the bedroom doors were closed. At one end were the steps leading to Benjamin and Helen's addition, at the other the stairway going down to the kitchen.

In the kitchen everything was ready for morning: the dishes were drying beside the sink, the counters had been wiped clean, the coffee-maker had been loaded with water and David's favourite blend.

David switched on the machine.

Amazing—only a few minutes ago he had thought he was going to die. Now, as the kitchen filled with the aroma of fresh coffee, he felt thirty again—full of energy and power, ready to face anything.

Suddenly hungry, he went to the refrigerator. In the meat compartment he found what he was looking for, smoked ham from a Kingston delicatessen. Then an added bonus: in the refrigerator door a row of bottles of the dark imported beer Helen always bought him without being asked. He pulled out a beer, ham, hot mustard, tore away some leaves of dark green lettuce. Soon he was sitting at the table, a feast piled in front of him, trembling with hunger.

"So this is what you do at night."

Bronski, unheard, had come in.

"Help yourself," David said. Amazing how clear his voice sounded, clear to the point of being transparent. But since his stroke everything had been like that—clear and transparent. His conversations with Melanie, his students, even Ruth and Benjamin, had taken on the quality of little plays, like the dramas Melanie used to arrange for her school. When they had all spoken their lines there was a little intermission while the scenery was changed, then a new exchange began. Eventually they would get to the last act, which would be his death. An event which—given his age and health—would cause no surprise or regret to anyone, least of all Melanie. Who now played her role in the comedy by urging him to take care of his health—as though his health were a stray dog that could be fed, shampooed, brought to new life.

Now Bronski, the Angel of Death, had arrived in time for the climax. He was not, as tradition would have it, wearing a hood. In fact he was dressed in pyjamas with a huge sweater drawn over. Unshaven, his face looked large and ominous. In front of him he was gradually, clumsily, building his sandwich. He had also, like David, discovered the beer.

"You couldn't sleep?"

"My body is still on European time."

"We're so glad you could come." The host who invites Death to his home must welcome him when he arrives.

"I am the one who is happy."

"And also Melanie."

Bronski nodded. He was holding a knife and trying to manoeuvre it in the mustard jar. David looked at his own hands. Tanned. Complete. White moons of his nails reassuringly pale against his darker fingers. Jakob Bronski's hands—or what was left of them—were not tanned. The skin was multicoloured, bruised for ever by what had happened, irregularly carpeted by sproutings of wiry black hair.

There was before the stroke and after the stroke, but sometimes David forgot where he was. Before the stroke he was always hungry and thirsty. He ate and drank as he pleased. Excellent appetite, as the vet used to say about various animals. The problem was that he no longer found himself very hungry. First of all, his mouth no longer worked properly. For a month one side of his face had been paralysed; even after the movement came back, the muscles of his cheek and jaw started to slacken when he was tired. A few bites and he began to feel as though he were at an exercise class.

"A few bites and I feel as though I am at an exercise class," he said to Jakob Bronski.

He looked across at Bronski. The skin around his eyes was the colour of dark clay.

"Between us," said Bronski, "I loathe exercise. There was a series of articles in a Moscow newspaper about the American love of running. Even the factory workers run at lunchtime, the article said. Can you imagine that? Also that there are special shoes—"

"Running shoes," David supplied.

"There was a boy in our flat. He made me promise to send him a pair of such shoes. Do you think we could?"

"Of course. But we would have to know his size."

"In my suitcase I have drawings of his feet."

Bronski ate slowly, deliberately, hugely. When he was part-way though his second sandwich he went to the refrigerator and took out two more of the imported beers. As Bronski walked, David thought how bandy and bowlegged were Bronski's legs, thin curved legs gradually sagging under the weight of that huge midriff.

"You don't eat?"

"No."

"You drink?"

"Please."

"You want to know why I eat so much? Because I am stubborn. Because I decided to become as large as possible so that it would take them a long time to starve me to death."

David made his face try to smile.

"I envy you," Bronski said.

"Our life is easy."

"Not that—I envy you living out your life with someone you love."

Despite himself David heard a strange sound escape his mouth, a sound that started as a sigh and ended as a groan.

"No? You don't?" Now Bronski's dark face had softened. David felt himself sighing again, letting out the breath he must have been holding ever since Bronski had sat down across from him. How could he have been afraid of this man? His face so vulnerable, so ugly, so battered by failure and pain.

"No."

Bronski nodded.

"I'm sorry to disappoint you."

Still, Bronski stayed silent, his face a slowly changing map onto which any country might still be inscribed.

"Did you know I used to be an expert on the ways Canadians died in France during the First World War? You know how the Jews died in France, I know about the Canadians. Between us we could do graveyard tours."

Bronski continued to look blank, and then suddenly he laughed. The sound took David so by surprise that he too began laughing. But the more he laughed the worse he felt, because the more he laughed, the wider opened the wound inside him—a wound unknown to him until this moment but now pushing tears through his eyes.

Bronski ate. Chewing slowly, reflectively, using both hands to work his sandwich into his mouth.

And David, the possibly dying Professor Doctor David Winters, reached for one of Bronski's cigarettes. Suddenly saw his hand frozen in space, reaching for another cigarette—fifty years before—reaching for a cigarette while—once again—fighting down tears. That had been 1938, in Vimy. He had been a pompous little scholarship student from Canada, a terrified Toronto Jew come to dip his toe in Nazi Europe—under the guise of doing research not on the war to come but the war that had already happened. From his listening post in France he had pressed his ear to Germany. Heard the sounds he was afraid to hear. Magnified his fear by going back to the sites of the battles of the Great War. Looked at the scarred landscape, the towns still part rubble, the trenches which rain and artillery had turned into mass graves. "The past is terrible," he had pontificated to his young man's diary, "but even more fearful than the past is the future." He had written that sentence—and many others like it—while sitting in a café, a glass of wine by his hand. With each swallow of wine the timescape grew darker, until finally—peering through a scarlet fog of prescience—he saw the future: a terrifying but none the less romantic battlefield that he, the historian, would eventually render into orderly paragraphs and explanations. Had he looked longer and more carefully, he would have seen Bronski struggling in the background. Bronski attracted to the same battlefield. Bronski snared, Bronski reduced to a skeleton, Bronski rebuilding himself with the same stubborn appetite he applied to building his sandwich.

It was possible, more than possible, that in half a century he, David Winters, scholarship student, frightened Toronto Jew, would-be and has-been eminent Canadian historian, had done nothing more than describe a complicated circle around this one arbitrary gesture: a hand extended across a table.

*7. The Gravity of Love: Flying without Wings,*
*the Advantages and the Disadvantages; Wherein,*
*Having Introduced the Reader to a Variety of Numerical*
*Concepts, the Author Attempts to Show How Newton's*
*Laws Are Brought into Play. The Application*
*of Newton's Law of Universal Gravitation—the Force*
*between Any Two Bodies Is Directly Proportional to*
*the Product of Their Masses and Inversely Proportional*
*to the Square of the Distance between Them; and*
*the Consequences of Newton's Third Law of Motion—*
*For Every Action There Is an Equal and Opposite Reaction.*


In Bronski's room, the universe had become a list of names.
Babovitch, Dimski, Garbov, Karpov, Leibowitz, Pagolini, Ne-
dayev, Limnit, Ben David, Tabowitz, Fogel, Landski, Faarn-
dow, Pippel, Lipschitz, Bender, Tarnow, Vogel, Mankiewicz,
Bebel, Zendel, Piakowski, Garber, Glade, Gimmel, Glad-
owitz, Horowitz, Garnowitz, Dahl, Dimmel, Dexter, Demeter,
Davidowski, Paskett, Trujillo, Derndl, Dagwood, Doge, Dao,
Tao, Tully, Tuske, Avraams, Abramovitch, Abrams, Aaronfeld,
Glube....

Like sheep jumping fences they were conjured forth: Darrell, Farrell, Errol, Beryl, Damian, Dimpel, Rasputin, Salutin, Isaac, Isaiah, Yitzhaak, Levi, Levitan, Lendl, Linnaeus....

With some he had attended Hebrew School in Warsaw, others had been his classmates at the university, soulmates in Russia, martyrs he had never met at Drancy but whose names he had memorized at the beginning; there were characters in books or plays, authors whose books he had never read, names he had invented because their sound appealed. And then there were the names of his fellow inmates at the mental hospital, the names he had recorded in his Red Cross notebook at Drancy. The names of the Red Cross workers themselves: Brossy, del Busso, a certain Marie-Joseph Brougeyre he had met only once but remembered because she had large soulful brown eyes which stared at him so relentlessly that he realized—absurd—that she must desire him, and even as they bent together over his lists of what the various inmates weighed—weekly records showing two-, five-, even sometimes ten-kilo losses until, given that the subject remained in camp and alive, the losses were reduced to those tiny negative increments a starving skeleton can shed— Yes, Marie-Joseph Brougeyre: there were times he had imagined himself spirited away on the flying carpet of Marie-Joseph, nestled in the dimpled downy arms of Marie-Joseph, suspended in the large soulful oceans of Marie-Joseph, inscribed in the new testament of Marie-Joseph. Marie-Joseph Brougeyre, *nota bene*, reminded him that even after the loss of his own family, his own kilos, what he had taken to be his own soul, the obscene demon within him still lived, the inescapable homunculus of vanity greed desire....

In the afternoon he had slept briefly while through the window had blown gentle breezes, the clicking of insect chatter, the melodies of birds flying contentedly from tree to tree. In the afternoon sleep had beckoned, but now it did not. After the music he had climbed into bed and stretched between Melanie's luxurious sun-smelling sheets, he had wriggled his feet and thought his legs, for once, felt like the legs—or at least the memory of the legs—of a young man. Full of motion and blood, pleasantly tired without aching. And he had stretched out in the bed with all his limbs extended to their utmost for the sheer pleasure of feeling the massage dance had given to his muscles.

But sleep had not come. Eventually he had gone downstairs—eaten, drunk, filled himself to bloating. Now, in bed once more, welcoming the waves of cool air that rolled in through the screen, it was no longer Babovitch, Dimski and Garbov, Karpov, Leibowitz and Pagolini. Not even Marie-Joseph, Melanie and Anna. Just himself, Jakob Bronski, on the altar of the new world, waiting for sleep to carry him away.

But sleep carried him nowhere. Sleep failed to arrive. Every few minutes one of his calves got a cramp, or an aching thigh had to be raised and lowered, or the place in his back which mysteriously flared up for months at a time began to hurt so much he had to sit up in order to shift the weight away.

Three o'clock in the morning and he was propped up in an uncomfortable bed in the middle of a strange continent. Three o'clock in the morning and his muscles were twisting in agony because they were stretched out on this ridiculous rack. He had already got up to go to the bathroom, splashed his face with water, swallowed aspirins. Recited his names, massaged his legs, taken his tour through the castle of memory bowing before locked doors. When morning came he would be tired, his stomach upset from the aspirin. To calm his stomach he would eat too much, the food would make him drowsy, he would sleep all afternoon and in twenty-four hours would be staring into the night again. Whereas, for example, had he never left his own apartment in Moscow—or, better, if he were in Paris now—the day would already be well established. Cafés would have been open for hours. Somewhere he could be sitting at a polished table, head down over a newspaper, drinking a chain of espresso coffees, smoking cigarettes strong enough to tear at the lungs.

On such a morning, at such a time, in such a place, he might even consider a small glass of cognac. Or a shot of calvados, for example. A tiny glass of grappa. Even a thimble of Sambuca served burning with coffee beans on top. Calvados, grappa, Sambuca. His half-brother, Stefann, had been an encyclopaedia of strong drink. When he had money he used to lead Jakob from one bar to the next, expert on the specialties of the house, the regions of origin of the liqueurs, the anecdotes surrounding their use. One two three—a dozen: Stefann could drink distilled alcohol the way Jakob could drink glasses of water. Burning his way into the night until finally the alcohol rendered him immobile, polished, his face smooth and glistening. Yes, Stefann had known how to drink into the night; Jakob had learned only the trick of taking one shot in the morning.

A Paris morning, to be exact, and it was Stefann who had taught him to expand the moment by swallowing the small dose that could burn through the haze of sleep, tobacco, coffee, burn a clear space through which the day would take on perfect clarity, glow briefly, shimmer above the ground and then simply float away. Until, at least, the occupation made such stupid pleasures impossible. After which there were no pleasures at all until Gabrielle.

Jakob tried to adjust the pillow under his back. Through the window moonlight spilled weakly into the room. He could see the pale square of the window, the outlines of desk and dresser, the peaks made by his feet beneath the blankets. As a child he had always slept with the shutters closed, absolute darkness, but at his uncle's farm moonlight had pierced through large cracks in the walls. Awake, afraid, listening to the night sounds of that wilderness where thunderstorms, pogroms, convolutions of history might at any moment tear apart the night, the shards of moonlight through those cracks had made him think of the steel of marching weapons. Sharp, crystalline, dangerous: to be able to sleep he had finally made himself slide his hands into the metal of that light.

After the music they had sat around the kitchen table, everyone's face red with pleasure. And then he had found himself leaning over his cup, staring into the dark coppery surface of his tea—unable to hear the voices of the others.

"You want to go upstairs?" He had let Melanie help him to bed. In a strange way she reminded him of Anna. Why not?

Of course her teeth were fixed and her hair was all one colour, but there was something sharp inside her—something Anna had taught him to recognize. Of that sharpness his wife had had nothing. Gabrielle had been only a girl—vulnerable, open-hearted, believing the best of everyone. Elementally, chemically innocent. Not for ever, of course. Not after they had taken her on her own train; in the days or weeks that followed she must have learned the way fear, death and indifference were the real underpinnings to what she had once called their castle of love. But no doubt in the end she hadn't even worried about herself. In the end, coughing out her ration of gas, she was probably trying to comfort whatever children were with her, holding them close, singing them into sleep with that high ethereal voice she had used to comfort their own daughter.

"How do you find us?" Melanie had asked him.

He had been sitting on the side of the bed, wearing the pyjamas Melanie had given him— "How do I find you?" He paused as if considering the answer. "Well, I find you well," was all he had been able to say.

Now he wished he had said more. About Christopher, for example, his shepherd from the old world to the new. Sweet, sly, spying Christopher and his father had been brought in only a week after Bronksi. The boy, thin and dreamy. The father, a wide blustery man always taking notes, interviewing, demanding answers. One morning the father was gone but Christopher remained. No explanations. No reaction from Christopher, who simply sat in his corner waiting his turn until Bronski forced him to eat, to follow him around, to become his "assistant" in charge of locating other stray children. After all those years, he could have said to Melanie, there was a part of Christopher still waiting. But in the wide and overfed body of the man something once soft and dreamy had tightened up. Biology, time, loss, had turned the boy into a man. And inside the man the sweet sly spying boy still hovered, taut as steel wire.

In Melanie, too, the girl still lived. Or so he would have liked to tell her. So she would have wanted to hear. Fearful and nervous. But sweeter than she had been. Sweet, beautiful, round

146

of soul. Through your eyes shines a soul that is round, he should have declared. Your round soul rises in the morning like the sun.

Neither sweet nor round, Anna's soul had been jagged, like her teeth. Nor had it been warm: searing heat alternating with icy cold that tore at the skin of your fingers and your lips. "You take your tea without milk? No wonder they shipped you to this place." Those were the first words she spoke to him. He hadn't thought Anna beautiful at first. A middle-aged woman strangely lopsided. Her dark hair with a fistful of white on one side; and her teeth—jagged already—had one eyetooth longer than the other. A small sharp fang, you could say. And that was the side of the mouth she grinned with, too. "If I were your angel could you wrestle me down?" she had asked him the next day. Not asked him, but hissed into his ear as they stood in line waiting for food. He had thought she was on the kind of drugs they gave the women sometimes. Then at night you would hear them moaning with the guards, and in the mornings their mouths would be bruised.

Right now he could hear the wind rising and falling in the leaves. Rubbing them together in the darkness, whistling through their secret places, then letting them lie still—

Your soul is like a sun, he should have said to Melanie, but he had been too tired to think or speak. In the morning he would assure her of this. Other flattering details. Your soul is like the sun, your eyes like stars, your hands like— In the game of love, in the game of reassurance, everything was like something else, something better, something that death couldn't touch. In the morning he would begin to play those old games, make lists of tasks for her to do, tell her stories to lead her from one day to the next.

He hadn't answered Anna. You don't answer women who are going to be fodder for the guards. One day he had been in the machine shed working on an old tractor and a guard had offered—nodding his head at one such woman as she passed— "You can change her oil if you like. A man is a man, after all, I understand."

147

He had pulled his hand out from the tractor engine. His good hand, relatively speaking, black with grease up to the elbow, a small bubbly trail of blood leading from a scraped knuckle. "Change her oil," Jakob had repeated, looking at his greasy arm and then pointing to the blood on his knuckle. The guard had laughed until he started coughing and had to spit.

The next morning Anna had not appeared with mouth bruised, hollow eyes, hateful complicitous looks at the guards. Not until dinner did he find her. Then she slid onto the bench beside Jakob and poked him in the ribs. "Wake up! How can we eat this slop? The dictatorship of the proletariat demands an end to back-kitchen Trotskyism—"

"Quiet."

"I'm starting a petition. In this model asylum for comrades who have fallen to the psychoses of revisionism — "

"Big words," Jakob said. She wasn't attractive. Only irresistible. Like a contagious disease you were eager to catch because it was exciting.

Rumours circulated: that she had been planted to test the inmates; that she was a disgraced minor Party official from some obscure town; that she was a cousin of the director; that she was the daughter or wife of some Politburo member, a woman who'd had influence, a golden tongue, perhaps even an affair with someone at the highest level—now being hidden away, perhaps being "taught a lesson". Meanwhile she was a self-declared thorn determined to scratch right through to the bone. After a week of taunting everyone with her gibberish slogans she pinned a message to the wall.

Guards, patients, victims, unite!
Throw off consciousness! Bark like dogs!
All those in favour of a revolution against the bourgeoisie
of medical imperialism join together at sunset! Like
Joshua we will howl until the walls between us
collapse and the true stateless dictatorship of the
people is born to our joyous embrace!

Jakob swung out of bed, went over to the dresser to get himself a cigarette. The match burned its small cave in the darkness. The way Anna's arrival had burned into the routine and boredom of the hospital. Of course her message was unsigned, but everyone knew who must be responsible for the raggedy sheet of paper flapping like a spoiled child's rebellion against the wall. That evening it was he who took the initiative. He sat down beside her. The first week she had gone about in her own clothes but tonight she was wearing one of the dull blue-grey cotton shirts patients were issued. In it she looked not more like the others but less—a rich girl dressed for a party with the peasants; although she'd donned the costume, she'd been unable to resist setting it off with a heavy jewelled necklace. As he leaned towards her, he noticed her skin was dark and velvety, glowing like the scientifically nourished pelt of a prize animal.

"Idiot," he said.

"Coward," she replied.

Later she would explain to him. Later she would insist—as though her idea were new—that every state enslaved the minds of its citizens in order to survive, that the only free country was the one beyond the borderline of fear, that "sanity" was only bureaucrat-speak for "sleep", that only flights into madness supplied strength. "Garbage," Bronski would protest, "we are oppressed because the state has weapons and we do not." Later—later they would spend hours elaborating in words what was obvious enough when he said, "Idiot," and she replied, "Coward."

Later, even later, when her blood was still visible on the concrete steps of their model institution, Jakob would realize that their brief idyll had been made possible only by the complicity of the guards. More than that? Definite orders from a higher-up to allow the affair to happen?

Yes, she had turned out to be a big fish after all—a fish that had to be baited. Making Anna bite must have seemed no problem: her sharp teeth, her over-developed fang, her unbalance, her rage, her unpredictable appetite must have already got her into trouble more than once. That was, after all, why she found herself here—even if it was a model institution.

Jakob—the morsel she was to be offered—arrived on a different road. No castoff from previous glory, no former official who might tell dangerous things to the wrong people, not even a Jewish revisionist who could disappear without comment, Jakob was someone who had slipped through the net, a translator who had caught the public eye and couldn't be destroyed without excuse, a potentially valuable talent that might gradually be domesticated. A patient that the director—coming from Jakob's last place of internment—had noticed and made follow him as a tame technician. Someone who might be useful as a helper in the long run, or easy to sacrifice in an emergency. How was he to know that Jakob would betray him by smuggling out those poems? Or that the poems would cause one of those international ripples that make it impossible to cauterize the wound?

A few days after the first notice, a second followed. Again, no retribution. Just a tension, an uncanny quiet. More rumours, too, in the men's dormitory. Comrade Anna had been brought in to test them. Comrade Anna was charged with promoting a rebellion so that those who co-operated might be shot. Of course anyone could be drugged, exiled, taken away without explanation at any time. Transferred to another institution because space had become available. But since Anna's arrival the hospital seemed to have entered a state of suspended animation. There had been no other new arrivals. No transfers out. Therapy and work continued but the oppressive hand of authority seemed to have lightened. To be suspended in the air, waiting for its chance to thunder down.

In her third notice Anna referred to the "well-known sexual perversions of Our Leader". The next morning she was taken from the women's dormitory, returned that evening comatose and unable to move. Jakob went to see her. She was lying on her bed, her head twisted to one side, as though it were a heavy ball about to roll onto the floor. He went to her, adjusted it on the pillow. Her eyes were closed, the lids dark and swollen with blood. Underneath were thick brown circles. She was breathing slowly, heavily, like a draft horse fallen between its traces. As she breathed a thin stream of spittle formed on her chin.

Both sides of her neck had small cuts, as though her necklace had been torn off. Later he would discover it was she who had ripped it free.

"You see," Jakob said to himself, "who could she be that they would do this to her?" He knelt beside her, wiped her face clean. At the door a woman known as Dr. Lydia watched him. Dr. Lydia was a former staff member who had somehow fallen into being a patient. The only sign of her former status was that she lived in her own room, a cupboard beside the laboratory; aside from possibly spying, she seemed to have no remaining duties.

"She's dead," Dr. Lydia now said. Barely taller than a dwarf, heavy black moustache, strong discoloured teeth that showed too much when she talked, as though she wanted her words to bite the listener.

"No she's not." He pulled her eyes open, expecting to find them unconscious. Instead, as he put his hands to Anna's eyelids, she opened them herself, winked at him.

"Are you going to sleep with her?"

"Yes," Jakob said. "Would you mind turning out the light?"

"Very funny. How does a Jew get into a place like this?"

"How does a Jew get out of a place like this?" Jakob replied automatically. He rolled up Anna's sleeves. There were marks where they had injected her on the insides of both elbows. One scab was almost as large as a coin: that one must have been expertly done. He wondered if her injections had been given in the director's office, where he had received his, a series that lasted for months. That was after he had picked up a guard and thrown him into the side of a bulldozer. He could still remember the look of outrage and surprise on the man's face as his back smashed into the iron blade — then he had fallen to the ground, paralysed. No other guards were present and Jakob had gone to the director's office to announce what he had done. "You were in shock," the director said at once, then strapped Jakob down on the big leather-covered table. Whatever had led up to the incident, whatever else followed, the series of shots had permanently erased. He could only remember the guard's stupefaction as he fell, the director's face as he leaned over him, day after day, a curiously benevolent smile as he pressed the needles home. And the interviews afterwards, supposed therapy sessions. It was Jakob, of course, whose English translations of the director's theories had brought him a small article in an American psychiatric journal. At the time, a time when Soviet psychotherapy was being ridiculed in the West as a cross between nineteenth-century Pavlovism and incomprehensible Marxist garble, the director's paper on "Social Schizophrenia East and West" made a favourable impression. But after the incident with the guard, the director no longer discussed social schizophrenia with Jakob. Instead, the door to his office locked, he pulled out a chess-board and a bottle of black-market vodka. The official report, he told Jakob at the end of the sessions, was that the guard had been alone in the shed at the time of the incident, and had slipped and fallen due to the fact that he had been drunk on illegally obtained alcohol. Eventually the director gave Jakob further material for translation.

"You're staring." Dr. Lydia was kneeling beside him, slapping his face lightly.

Jakob shook his head. In those days, less than two years since his own injections, he still sometimes drifted off.

"They gave them to her here, too." Dr. Lydia took off the blanket, lifted up Anna's skirt, showed Jakob a scab on her hip. She was wearing fancy semi-transparent underpants which showed the dark shadow of her pubic hair. Jakob felt a sudden burst of confusion. Tenderness, disgust, pity, mixed together. He reached quickly to pull the skirt down, but couldn't help letting his fingers brush against her thighs as he did. Hating himself even as her warm skin burned into his fingers.

The next morning, when Jakob came up to see her, Anna's eyes were open. "Death to the mind police," she managed weakly. He sat beside her on the bed. She took his hands, held them as though everything had already been decided, had already happened.

"Idiot," he said.

"Coward." She was smiling, everything about her—from her uneven teeth to the scar he now noticed at the corner of her mouth—fixed him, hypnotised him, evaded his defences and went straight for— For what? She held his hands. He was wrong. She wasn't trying to attack him. She was making an offer: unconditional total love. It was there, spread between them, a new geography she had invented and in which, he realized, he had been living since the moment he walked in the door.

He withdrew his hands to roll a cigarette. A grin was breaking out on his face. He tried to mask it by sticking out his tongue to lick the paper. As he squinted the light in the room grew brighter. He looked at Anna. She was looking back at him. They edged closer on her bed, adjusting their bodies to the immense gravity of love.

She giggled, she pushed her hair back from her forehead, she stared at him for a long time without blinking.

When her eyes were on his face he felt it could explain itself. When they stopped at his shoulders he saw them moving from side to side, taking in the weight, the muscle, the twist where the dislocation had been. Ten years of hard labour—he had been strong then, much stronger than now: trees, rocks, machines—he had wrestled them all, tested himself against them, used them to get stronger for the day he would explode. Because he believed in that then—explosions—believed in his own desire to grow so strong that his explosion would tear apart—but what? There was nothing he was strong enough to destroy—except himself. In the camps there were others, too, who built and conserved their rage. Against the day when the rages of the oppressed would unite and overthrow—but whom? But how? The armed might of the state was the beat of a million drums against the feebleness of their childish whispers. In the end, he began to think, in the end he was as he had been born—a Jakob, waiting for God to send him His angels.

Her eyes crossed his shoulders, his chest, his belly and groin.

Later he would tell her everything, for now they were continents finding their places on their new planet. He had failed to change the world. She also had failed there. He had failed to find a perfect moment to die. She also was alive. Imperfect, penitent, unforgivable, absolved. Dr. Lydia was in the doorway. She was smiling, radiant, a midwife present at the birth. "You won't be disturbed," she said. She closed the door behind her.

A trap? A plot? A connived contrivance?

His heart was pounding. Without knowing it he had crushed his cigarette on the floor, wrapped his hands around Anna's waist.

"Do we trust her?"

"Death to the mind police."

For a moment there must have still been time to go back; but the moment dried up and blew away.

"Are you going to sleep with her?" Dr. Lydia had asked. But he had never asked Anna and she had never asked him. They had taken each other anywhere and any way they could. In the animal stalls, in the machine shed, in the director's private bathroom; in their hands, in their mouths, in their hair; in trust, in love, in vain, in desire, in desperation, in place of everything else they couldn't possess. For twenty-four days, which he didn't count at the time but calculated later, searching for something to hold onto and ending up with nothing but a number and the necklace which she had—on that first night they tortured her, but not the last—in her extreme of pain, torn from her neck and gripped because she had decided that giving him this necklace was going to be her means of surviving the needles.

The number, the necklace and the reasonable certainty that she had told him, twice, "when I'm with you I'm not afraid to die."

Another match, another cave of light, another cigarette. The blood was thundering through him, a convoy of heavy trucks powering down narrow roads. He sat up, pushed his hair back, finally switched on a light. In Moscow when he couldn't sleep he would often get out of bed, read all night or work on his translations. In the corner of the room Melanie had placed the two small cardboard cartons that were supposed to contain his future in the new world. There were, she had explained, books to inform and entertain; also documents and testimonials of Jews who had suffered in Soviet Russia. A Toronto rabbi had supplied these—he was hoping that Jakob might be willing to help his people by translating, condensing, preparing speeches on the injustices suffered—

On top of the cartons was a small packet of letters. The one from Rabbi Goldman was written in Hebrew. Jakob scanned it. Was this supposed to be a joke? He recognized a few words: peace, his name, please. At the end of the letter the rabbi had appended a note in English: *Please forgive the fact I cannot write to you in Russian. However, I am studying, and perhaps you will hear from me in that language later this winter.*

A second letter was from the Canadian Jewish Congress inviting him to a conference. He would be on a panel, they suggested, on "The Meaning of Jewish Suffering". This letter also had a postscript, also handwritten: *You were in one of those hospitals. You have seen, you have suffered, you are a Jew and a poet. Tell the whole world what you know and the world will listen.*

He looked at the other letters from the Congress, put them aside, then held the final letter in his hand. The one with his name handwritten, and PERSONAL printed beside the name. This would be from Leah Goldman. He looked for the stamp but it must have fallen off, and the postmark was blurred. She would not be asking him to be on a panel or make a speech. Perhaps she had sent him an envelope full of dirty suggestions. Or more likely one of those notes he sometimes got from journalists after the poems were published, thank-you missives designed to leave a sweet taste.

He opened the envelope.

Dear Jakob Bronski,

I am writing you on a strange mission but perhaps you will understand when I have explained myself.

My legal name is Nadine Santangel. However, the name of my father is Jakob Bronski. If you are not he, I hope you will forgive my disturbing you. The Jakob Bronski who was my father married my mother Gabrielle Santangel on March 15, 1941 in Paris. Exactly six months later, on September 15 of that year, I was born. I could enclose a photograph of the three of us on the steps of our apartment building in Paris (I also have the marriage certificate and two letters of congratulations) but in the likely event your name is simply a coincidence, I desist.

Shortly after my birth, as I understand it, Jakob Bronski and my mother decided to attempt to flee to Spain. I was left behind with my mother's sister, Léonie Santangel, and under her care survived the war. In the meantime Jakob Bronski and his wife, Gabrielle, were identified as Jews, and taken off the train. The death of Gabrielle Santangel at Auschwitz-Birkenau was recorded, and therefore there is no possibility she survived. I thought the same about Jakob Bronski but a few years ago, when my aunt, Léonie Santangel, investigated, she was surprised to discover that in fact there was no record of Jakob Bronski's death, though he was known to have been interned at Drancy, outside of Paris.

Two years ago—if we ever meet I will be glad to explain to you why it took me so long—I became involved with the problems of Jewish emigration from Russia. Through this I met a certain Rabbi Goldman in Paris, who provided me with lists of Jews wishing to emigrate from Russia. It was on one of these lists that I found your name; by the time I wrote him to ask your address, you had, according to Rabbi Goldman, already left Moscow for the address to which I have sent this letter.

I know from Rabbi Goldman that you spent a few days in Paris, and therefore I know that you did not go to see Léonie Santangel, the sister-in-law with whom my father left his child. Once that would have made me believe that you could not be my father. Now, I know otherwise.

The man who was my father had a stepbrother, Stefann Piakowski. He came to Canada after the war and established himself as an astronomer at the University of Toronto. A few years ago he died, after a long and successful career.

Due to his influence and help, I also resettled in Toronto, where I still live. Also with his help, I became a professor of astronomy at the University of Toronto, a post I held until my recent marriage. Without children, I add hastily, for in the case that you are my father you would undoubtedly want to know whether you are also a grandfather.

Whoever you are, I hope your life here is a good one. And, whoever you are, whatever your reasons, I hope you will get in touch with me.

Yours sincerely,

Nadine Santangel (née Bronski).

Holding the letter required both his hands. And even gripped by both his hands, or what remained, the sheet of paper fluttered and stuttered in the night, seemed to want to wrench itself free and fly away. Underneath her name was an address, trembling too violently to be read, and a telephone number. In his blood the sound of heavy traffic had grown more intense. If he lay down now, he knew, he would die. *The immense gravity of love*, yes, but now what he felt was not love but an unbearable storm inside.

He managed to get on his clothes. Out of his pants pockets he emptied his roubles, his francs, his dollars; from now on the letter was the only currency he would be needing. And then, switching off his light, he eased his way out of the bedroom, downstairs, through the kitchen door and into the night.

The air outside was alive with tiny currents, insects, odours of fields and nearby barns. For a moment he felt calmed, as though all he had needed was to escape the dead zone of the house. Then, even as his eyes adjusted to the darkness, the gigantic archings of trees fully leaved, the grey barns looming up from ground's blackness, the clamour inside began again. A mosquito had caught itself in the hair above one temple. It whined and buzzed until he pressed his hand against his skull and squashed it.

Moving forward, now, he crossed the grass between the house and the barn, then let himself in through the office door. He could smell the fresh-cut hay stored above, a sweet throbbing odour that made him want to cry.

The moon shone directly through the office window onto the desk. Opening the drawer he withdrew one of the boxes he had found that afternoon. He shook out the cartridges, then stood them on their flattened ends so they shone like rows of silver rockets.

For a moment it was enough to see these rows, inhale the thin smell of their metal power cutting through the thick fragrance of hay and animal. Then, from the cupboard, he took out the rifle. It broke open easily. He blew out the chambers, pulled his shirt-tail from his pants to clean them.

Now he opened the door that separated the office from the barn. The cattle were breathing noisily, slow grinders chewing away the night.

When he went in he was greeted by a series of grunts, soft moanings, heavy thuds as the cattle, aware of him, began working their way to their feet. Jakob stood still, talking in a low voice:

Through the windows above the stalls moonlight sent a grey-silver glow. Enough light to make little masterpieces of the dust-filled cobwebs stretched across the panes. Enough to see the beams of the barn, the outlines of the stalls, the curious reflections of bovine eyes.

One white face was slung over the top board of its stall, and staring constantly at Jakob.

Jakob moved close to the cow. She followed Jakob with her head as he came down the centre runway of the barn, leaned on the boards next to her. The moonlight picked out raw gougings in the wood: Jakob stared at them until suddenly he made out the letters J-U-L-I-E-T where David had carved them that afternoon.

A few stalls away, one of the cattle gave a long sigh, then eased itself down into the straw. The others followed suit; the barn was filled with the sounds of heavy bodies dropping onto the straw-covered cement floor, long plaintive sighs.

Still carrying the rifle, Jakob climbed over a slatted partition, lowered his feet carefully. "Could you be Juliet?" He reached out and plunged his fingers into the woolly hair of her belly. It was hot, fibrous, knotted. He rubbed his fingers, his knuckles, the skin of his palms into the rough fur. The cow sighed. Jakob ran his hands up to her spine. The big knobs of her backbone raised up humps of muscle and flesh. Jakob pushed his hands up her neck, fanned them out to grasp her horns. The cow twisted its head away from him, then swung it back quickly, hitting Jakob in the chest and sending him staggering back into the heavy elm boards.

At the hospital they had let him out with the animals. That had been after the blood and shock treatments, after the electricity had burned its special path through his brain. When he had recovered—or at least regained the ability to leave his bed for meals—the director had set him to doing a translation into English for an American visitor. "The former practice of prolonged isolation has been condemned," the director wrote, "since isolated patients tend to become wildly excited and aggressive." *Wildly excited and aggressive*; yes, there were occasions when these words could have been used to describe him. But the director had not chosen to explore the exact meaning of the word "isolated". He had not chosen, for example, to explain that a patient might feel "isolated" after decades of sexual and emotional deprivation, or, equally, after the sudden removal of—a loved one. "Wildly excited and aggressive", on the other hand—there, the director had elaborated. He had even given the history of a certain individual, a war refugee who after years of good behaviour had attacked a guard. Following this attack an experimental treatment had been attempted. As the editor of the American journal had noted in his preface: "Each experimenter, in accordance with the dialectic method, feels an obligation to present a theory, a rationale, for his approach." Thus the director had written about how, in the case of this certain individual, the dialectical opposites had been brought together by "emphasizing the internal contradictions". The first stage had involved "the deepening of the contradiction"—to be exact, the injection of incompatible blood. This stage had sent the patient into a coma from which he had been revived by matter in its purest form—to be exact, pure energy in the form of electricity. "Such experiments might eventually lead, through correlations of the patient's mass and the amount of electricity applied, to a quantifiable relationship between energy and psychosis," the director wrote. In the case of the certain individual, however, the experiment was discontinued when the life of the subject appeared to be in danger. The American editor had here introduced a footnote explaining the importance of electro-shock and pre-frontal lobotomy in the current five-year plan.

After making the new translation, Jakob had once more been allowed into the barn. Perhaps to break his isolation by encouraging him to make new friends among the sheep, the chickens, the cattle for whom he was caring. Caring with extreme care, moving slowly, every step measured as though he were wearing concrete boots, because for some reason the electricity had taken all the feeling away from his feet and he was always falling on his face. Until he made love with Anna.

On this subject there was also a paper from the director—in the form of one of Jakob's poems. It postulated that the inner heat of orgasm had acted like a heroic comrade with a welding torch, repairing the bridge of neurons leading to the soles of his feet—which therefore, as he came, first burst into flame, delicious agony. Then began to curl, pulse, cramp and throb—so overwhelming that he was barely aware of the rest of it—just a long crackling whisper as he spurted into her; and his seed also must have been on fire because it burned his sex as it passed, sent Anna into her own electro-frenzy of moans, neck-snapping, muscles trying to tear free from bones.

For weeks after, with every step he felt as though his naked feet were being caressed by the soil of Eden. Anna, too, walked as though reborn: even though she was able to keep the sullen mask on her face, she couldn't disguise the fact that her body seemed to have been reconstructed.

Until it was her turn for a second round of injections. The hospital was, after all, as the patients were continually reminded, an experimental facility they were privileged to be at. Complete with the latest treatments designed to rid them of everything from war traumas to political and moral schizophrenia. A country estate that had once belonged to a wealthy family. A self-supporting, in principle, farm: animals for meat and milk and wool, fruit trees from which jam could be made. A forest from which fallen trees and branches could be harvested to feed the stoves in winter.

During the period when his feet were numb he would go out and sit with the animals, listening to them breathe, matching his own breath to theirs. Hobbling up and down with pail and brush, he would count out the rhythms of his lungs.

After his feet woke up he still sought out the company of the animals, partly to avoid suspicion and partly because he preferred their company to the company of his fellows or his superiors.

Eventually Anna's sullen mask became her whole being once more, until she made the only escape she could—a bone-jarring, muscle-wrenching escape from the gravity of love into the gravity of death: a headlong leap from the roof onto the newly built cement steps leading to the double-glassed doors—the steps, wide and proudly curved, where a delegation of Party officials had posed with a recent tour of foreign psychiatrists. Jakob, after certain discussions possibly better termed interrogations, was assigned the task of scrubbing the steps clean. Scrubbing them every morning for 365 days, a full year, scrubbing them from seven to nine every morning in heat, in freezing cold, through ice, through rain; scrubbing when mosquitoes swarmed in the face and scrubbing on mornings so beautiful that he almost cried the tears he had resolved to hide. After this morning task Jakob would go to the barn, thrown back to his original reason: breathing, breathing with the animals, feeling the air move in and out of his lungs—life the tide, his body the shore with no choice but to accept until the tide receded for ever.

*8. Making Movies: The Big Bang, Part II*


He was sober. Why, he did not know, but sobriety had struck, arrived, invaded—whatever it is sobriety does, it had done it to him. Years ago, when the well was full, he had often written this way: an evening of drinking followed by a long sober night during which—dead tired, nerves raw—he could sit typing slowly but without stopping—word after word, sentence after sentence, paragraph after paragraph laboriously hammered onto the paper.

One year he had written six books that way, under three different names, never once typing fast enough to set up a real clatter. Not like now, for example, when he covered page after page with blinding speed, each one torn eagerly out of the machine and crumpled before being tossed over his shoulder.

From his luggage Christopher extracted the emergency second bottle of Glenlivet, unscrewed the top, took a sip. A few more sips, slurps, gulps, and he could sit down at the typewriter and start wasting paper. Or perhaps the moment had arrived for a new novel. Why not? He couldn't spend the rest of his life writing scripts for the old ones. On the other hand, perhaps film had become his form now—the Grandma Moses of the movie world, he would give birth to himself as an Anglo-French *auteur*, the one who had baptized himself just a couple of hours ago. Nothing could be more obvious. Even David must have seen it coming. Sarcastic bugger. Setting up a desk in the loft—putting out a typewriter, a sheaf of paper—why not a vase of roses? In the film David would knock over a vase of roses in the middle of the desert. And the *auteur*, poor sod, would be left with no recourse but to sneak off to his typewriter and communicate with the beautiful Melanie through the written word.

Christopher made a frame with his hands, the way he'd seen directors do it, and peered through it at the desk—trying to get the image of himself, the hero of his own movie. But another image intruded. The face of Jakob Bronski in the second photograph, the photograph that had appeared when his poems were published in the British newspaper. In that photograph the bones of his face had protruded like knuckles from a fist. One cheek puffed. Round steel spectacles. Thin nose broken at the bridge. Christopher had seen that happen: it was the morning Jakob Bronski was taken away from Drancy. Just as they were going through the gate he had thrown himself at one of the guards. He moves like a girl, Christopher had thought. And the guard hadn't even bothered to shoot him. Just deflected him with his elbow and lashed out with his boot, catching Jakob in the face.

That winter everyone was talking about the Liberation to come. Talking about it, afraid to talk about it, afraid that they would be shipped off to their death before the Americans came. New arrivals were eagerly quizzed for news. You could always recognize them: their hurts fresh, their bones still covered with flesh, their faces strangely open, attuned to wider places. Melanie's thin cold skin. Her white wrists sticking out of the oversize black sweater she got from—but now Christopher couldn't remember the woman's name; he could see the face, though, one of those stony elegant faces worn by well-to-do Frenchwomen in their fifties. Like someone in her own parlour she'd stripped off her sweater in the centre of the courtyard, then put her coat back on and handed the sweater to Melanie without a word. The funny way she breathed that winter, always with a cold. The feel, the sound, the smell of wet concrete. The grainy pitted surface that yielded bits of sand and dirt when your skin rubbed against it. The slow-drying stains left by rain, urine, buckets of slops. The vulnerable soft pad of naked feet against concrete floors. The cold sandpapery bite of concrete walls through four layers of clothes. The echoing slip-slop of torn-soled shoes. The harder metal echo of steel-toed boots, the heavy artillery sound of steel heels. Smells of sewers in the heavy rain. Standing among the men at the long metal urinal. Always shielding his uncircumcised member as he peed. The way dried blood on a concrete floor started as a dark crust, then turned bright red as you scrubbed—briefly reconstituted itself like powdered milk, so that while the victim's body might have been gone for days the blood was alive again, a little pool of bright hopeful red. Jakob Bronski's dry voice. His praying for them—first long impromptu addresses to God, then softly chanted Polish lullabies.

Jakob Bronski, cantata in bumpy sounds. Jakob Bronski, magical fellow out of some feudal fairy tale. Always darting about the courtyard. Up and down the stairs, in and out of every room, record book in one hand, would-be "doctor bag" filled with ersatz supplies in the other. Brown eyes snappy with flinty green streaks. Small round steel-framed lenses always about to take a slide down the long narrow nose. Wide mouth with modestly narrow lips. Not the lips of a glutton or a sensualist, rather the lips of an uncle you can trust not to swallow you up some hungry night. White skin. Hollow cheeks and bony forehead—but those were standard issue here. Fine hands: slim smooth fingers that, like the trustworthy mouth, inspired confidence, even love.

Jakob Bronski. In the movie he would be a puppet-maker. First escaped from the ghettos of Poland to France. Then from the starvation and beatings of Drancy to Auschwitz. And after Auschwitz? Worse, no doubt, horrors that only the puppet-maker museum would dare to catalogue. Whistling all the while, a busy saint making more survivor puppets wherever he went. Bronski the puppet-maker who used bones and flesh and frightened empty brains to turn out little neo-Bronskis—walking, talking semi-human amalgams that he had refitted in his jolly little toyshop, pure survivor dolls.

Christopher, not for the first time, had the unwanted vision of himself and Melanie as soulless projectiles launched at the world by their busy-fingered saviour. In the movie the puppet-maker would definitely steal the scenes. Perhaps the film would even open with the puppet-maker adrift in Paris before the war. With his trustable hands, his modest lips, his grim need to survive, he commits the first act of creation: he falls in love with a woman who would not otherwise have died. Of course, he knows the danger to which he is exposing her. Even if he doesn't know for himself—and as a refugee how could he not?—he has a yellow star on his coat to remind him. But the puppet-maker marries. The puppet-maker makes a baby. Then he abandons it. The night his new puppets are to leave for Auschwitz, the puppet-maker confesses that not only did he cause the death of a perfectly innocent wife, but he brought into the world a daughter who is also probably dead by now—a child whose very life was only a brief tribute to his monstrous ego.

Christopher was lying on his face on the carpet in the dark. He was remembering that Valentine's Eve at Drancy, Valentine's Eve 1944. He was wondering if—after all this time—he was finally discovering the obvious: that for the whole time some part of him—the most important part—had stayed behind in the room at Drancy where he had spent the night with Melanie Lansing believing they would be leaving on the death train the next day, consoling each other and being consoled by Jakob Bronski.

That night at Drancy he had been ready to die. Perhaps he had even wanted to die. Certainly, unlike other times there, he had had no thought of escape. No fantasies of leaping off the train, no imagined superhuman tussles with the guards. Ready to die with Melanie; their lights were to go out together and that would have been the end of the story.

His lips tasted of dust, his face was gritty. At Melanie's wedding he had got drunk like this. So drunk someone had had to take him to his hotel room. Eventually Melanie had come by to check on him. He had started drinking again. She'd taken the bottle away. Undressed him. Put him into bed. And then either he had fallen asleep or he hadn't. Either dreamed he was making or actually made love to her. Snippets remained: her fingers longer than he remembered from the desert, her face swollen and red, her mouth working, "Don't you see I *have* to marry him? Don't you *see*?" Next thing he knew he was standing in the shower, saying that no, he didn't see, but when he came out he was alone, still drunk, more drunk than he had ever been with the possible exception of tonight, so drunk he had had to get dressed, go down to the hotel bar, start drinking again until finally someone hit him. Christopher got to his feet, turned on a light.

He was drunk but he was sober. He was tired but he was awake. In the film the author would go to the Master and beg enlightenment. "I am tired when I am awake and awake when I am tired," he would say. "I am drunk when I am sober and sober when I am drunk. Release me from these contradictions."

"Only you can release yourself," the Master would say. He would be a ten-year-old Italian boy with a shaved head and twin gold rings through his left ear. CLOSEUP to face. Dark almond eyes, black pupils swimming in pure whiteness. The Master begins to weep blood. EYES FILL SCREEN. We see the Master is weeping not blood but armies of miniature ants.

"Give me wisdom, O Master," the frightened *auteur* says.

"Never eat in restaurants you can't afford." FADE to the *auteur* in a dark room, breathing heavily with his stomach. Then turning on the light.

In his hand was a bottle. Beneath his feet a dark oriental carpet. The centre of the room was occupied by a bed. The walls were lined with bookshelves, odd bits of furniture that must have been picked up at the auctions Melanie used to write him about. That had been amazing: waking up in Paris to the *clump* of duty-letters from Melanie outlining the life she was living with David in Toronto, their weekend forays to the country and the auction barns. Amazing to think of one of Bronski's survival puppets driving about in a station wagon trying to buy "authentic" knick-knacks.

Christopher gave the bottle a ritual tap. Sat down in front of the typewriter. "Last Will and Testament of Christopher Lewis," Christopher began. Lucy had always said he should have a will or otherwise his papers and letters would get picked over by whoever arrived first.

"If it's an open coffin," Christopher typed, "and, circumstances permitting, that is my preference, dress me in my best clothes. If necessary buy a new suit, a clean shirt, even a silk tie. Lucy Chadwick will supply the necessary funds. My favourite shoes are the black ones at the back of the closet that I never wear because I save them for special occasions."

Christopher arched his back, dug his fists into the flesh covering his kidneys, pushed. His back was sore, his insides felt sluggish and out of kilter. He stood up. Swaying back and forth he moved away from his desk towards the darkened edges of the room.

"Something I should read?"

He turned so quickly towards the unexpected voice that his feet got crossed and he fell over.

"Sorry. I didn't mean to frighten you. But I wanted to come to say goodnight. You were so terribly *drunk*, Christopher, I couldn't just leave you out here doing God knows—"

"Melanie—"

"I see you're—"

"—safe and sound."

She was sitting on the top step. Easy to see, now that his eyes had adjusted away from the bright glare of the desk lamp on white paper to the half light at the edges of the loft.

"You want me to help you up?"

"I'm fine." Christopher slid across the rug so that his back was supported by the bed. His ankle was throbbing and he reached down to massage it.

"Poor Christopher."

"And you—"

"Well—"

She tilted her head to one side, hair falling past her shoulder. The gesture of a young woman, the kind of gesture the actress would make in the film. But if this was the film, what scene would this be? The scene, Christopher thought, feeling suddenly calm and in control, when the author suddenly reveals to the heroine that what is happening is not life but a movie, that the thoughts, the words, the movements she takes to be her own have all in fact been scripted in order to balance the needs of art and commerce. Melanie was watching him, sitting comfortably on the top stair, her head still tilted. It was, he now remembered, the way she used to sit at Drancy. Strange, how memory dredged up images from the camp—but always of Melanie and Jakob. Of course there were others he remembered. Others who were sentenced to death from the very beginning. But he and Melanie, foreigners, began with the illusion that their stay was only temporary, that their cases were different, that their release was only a matter of days.

"You look well," Christopher said.

"Don't talk to me like—"

"What?"

"Condescending."

"You *do* look well. I think that place you go to must be some kind of health farm where they give you dirty massages."

"Very funny, Christopher. Typical evasive tactic. Every ten or twenty years or hundred years Christopher and Melanie get together. And do you know what we do?"

"You tell me."

"You get drunk, you pick a fight, you stumble off into the night and sulk."

"And you chase after me?"

"I need us to have something, Christopher. Don't you remember all the promises we made to each other? We were always going to stay close to each other. Be each other's family. Tell each other everything."

"I remember. Have you told me everything about yourself?"

"Of course not," Melanie said. She had straightened her head now, and her hands were laced together—another gesture he remembered from the camp. Also from the expedition, when she took him for a walk and told him she had taken David "as a lover".

"Tell me now," Christopher said. He was uncomfortable on the floor. He pushed himself up, lay down on the bed, propped his head up on his elbow. "I'm waiting."

"You know, Christopher, when we went driving this afternoon I was thinking to myself that you'd really changed. You seemed more—I don't know—Christopher, I don't even know if I should be telling you this."

"Tell me."

"Something about your face, Christopher. You seemed more human. But then tonight when you wandered off—I hate it when people get drunk."

Now she was bending towards him, her face oddly angled. In the movie this would be a close-up. Or perhaps not. Perhaps the camera should keep its distance, leave Melanie's large eyes glowing at the edge of the light.

"Are you drunk, Christopher?"

"No."

"You don't really know me any more, do you? But I think you care about me. I believe you do. Maybe more than anyone. Do you still want me to tell you my secrets, Christopher?"

"Yes."

A long wait. And then: "All right, Christopher. I'll tell you." Then she came and sat beside him on the bed. "You want to hold my hand?"

"Crazy girl." He was aware of Melanie's breath, of the rhythm of her breathing. At Drancy she had been so small, her breaths tiny whispers. But she had grown into a full-sized woman. Substantial. Flesh and bone. House and husband. Nuthouse and hospital. Worldwide lists of political prisoners and files spilling with carbon copies of her demands for justice. "Do you remember Drancy—that Valentine's Eve?"

"Yes, Christopher, I remember."

Her breath was on his face. He reached out. "Do you remember when you asked me to touch you?"

"Yes. Like now, Christopher. Touch me now."

She unbuttoned her blouse, took Christopher's hand, cupped it first around one breast, then, sliding it farther across in the darkness, against something hard and gravelled. A jolt of fear and his belly knotted, but he managed to keep his hand from jumping away.

"Cancer?"

"Yes."

"Why didn't you tell—"

"I just did."

He ran his hand over the scar. It was irregular. Massive. Ridges of hardened tissue extended up from where her breast had been to the lymph glands beneath her armpit.

"Old?"

"Almost two years."

"Melanie—"

"They say they got it." She paused. "Don't say anything right now. Please. Just swallow your tongue or count to a hundred." Without warning her hand slid inside his shirt. Something inside twisted away. "Do you still make love?"

"Sometimes."

"Do you have a girlfriend? A little missus stashed away in gay Paree?"

"Melanie, I can't make love to you. Not here."

"Why not?"

Her hand was on his belly, circling, stroking, waking muscles and nerves that had lain dormant for years. At this moment, in the film, it would be time to CUT TO NEXT MORNING where the writer and Melanie could be seen sitting at the kitchen table. Their faces—guilty? ecstatic? disappointed?—would fill out the story in a way no censor could object to. Unseen by the audience, for example, the awkward moment when belt and zipper were undone. The graceless attempts of ageing legs to wriggle out of tight waterlogged trousers. The unromantic grunt as a large and awkward body attempted a manoeuvre better suited to a twenty-year-old ballet dancer. Despite which he arrived on top of her. His eyes were closed. Inside she was scalding hot. He opened his eyes. She was smiling, but not exactly, and her lips and cheeks were swollen. Somehow she had got her thighs around his waist—she was squeezing hard, so hard the breath was leaving him. He put his hand to her mouth, she took it, bit into his wrist.

"Christopher." He was looking into her eyes, she was carrying him now, waking him up, repeating his name over and over again in this new voice of hers he had never heard; but even as his body began to move with hers, he couldn't help moving his hands and his lips onto the scar; Bronski had saved them from their first deaths so they could live out these others, the little deaths of sex, the deaths of cancer, of fear, of lives unlived—

"Christopher," Melanie said, but, shipwrecked by whisky and sex, Christopher had collapsed. Melanie knelt over him, feeling suddenly vulnerable and shy. She stretched her hand out gingerly, put it lightly on Christopher's chest to ride the rise and fall of his breathing, the thudding of his heart.

Amazing to see Christopher so *still*. But he was stillness now, dead calm. She stretched, she curled experimentally against him, then allowed her legs to tangle with his. The sounds of insects, birds, their own breathing, roared through the silvery air. But in the spaces between was an eerie and total silence, an absolute vacuum into which anything might be injected.

"Just swallow your tongue or count to a hundred," she said to herself. The way she had the night she first discovered David's infidelities.

That was at the farm: she was emptying his suit jacket for the cleaners when a thick letter fell from an inside pocket. David was in bed reading, apparently unaware of the catastrophe about to unfold. "Look at these stamps," Melanie remembered saying. "A French letter! David, you naughty boy." Hardly suspecting, even as David tried to grab it and she jerked it away—turning it over without meaning to, so that the photographs fell to the pine floor she had, on her knees, scraped free of paint and sanded and waxed to a glowing gold while David spent two weeks in France doing research for "Canadians in the Trenches during the Great War".

The pictures were of the woman David had found to keep him company in his own trenches. Her bathing costume, modest, did not hint at voluptuous charms. Rolled down to the waist, it merely displayed them. Otherwise his story about a researcher, a hot-day swim on the war-scarred beaches of Normandy, might have worked better. "Count to a hundred," Melanie instructed herself. Then was relieved to discover she was too clever to get angry right away. Too clever for anything but an interrogation disguised as a sermon against jealousy, a simple plea to know the truth because she was happy to be married to a man whose manliness extended beyond his family, beyond even the borders of his own country.

She managed to extract a certain number of details. For those evening hours, quizzing David as he drank whisky to ease the shock, she almost believed she wasn't jealous. And then when he fell asleep—relieved, ashamed—she went for the matches. "Count to a hundred," she was chanting. At first it was only the bed she was trying to ignite. When that didn't work she used crumpled newspaper as kindling and tried to set fire to the sheets, his clothes, the contents of his wallet and briefcase. Finally she got the curtains going. Thick lung-biting smoke filled the room. She held her breath, counting. David woke up coughing and retching, then finally spotted her across the room, crouched in the corner, wet cloth against her face, waiting for him to die.

Christopher's breathing had deepened and slowed. She kissed his forehead. Strange to be naked in this loft. Stranger yet to be naked with Christopher. Though it had almost happened at the wedding, in his hotel room. They had both been so drunk, and wrestled each other to the bed—not for sex but out of anger. Then he had passed out. Strange, weird, unprecedented, amazing to discover herself this way with Christopher; this universe, this Christopher-and-her universe must have been waiting for them all these years; they could have gone their whole lives without discovering it and yet, now that she had entered this state with him, she didn't know how she would ever leave.

She put on Christopher's shirt, crossed the dark loft to the desk. A page in the typewriter, cigarettes, a mostly full bottle. She read the beginning of the will, then took a pen and carefully drew chains of hearts around the words. Then she switched off the light. Through the window of the loft she could see the house rising out of the darkness.

When she turned back to the bed Christopher's eyes were open, two silvery discs pointed her way. Pinned: the silver discs had her pinned to the rough wool of the carpet. Christopher's shirt held her arms—oddly akimbo—like a straitjacket. "Don't look at me like that," she finally managed to say and when Christopher laughed, breaking the spell, she moved to kneel beside him.

He took her hand. "Loony tunes," he said. "Melodie Dancing." And then his free hand was on her back, a large meaty paw she could feel warming her ribs, sliding between breast and scar. "I still can't believe you kept this all so secret. You must have been terrified when they told you?"

"I don't know. It didn't happen that way—an announcement out of the blue. It was a few weeks after David's stroke, when he was home from the hospital, I was taking a shower and I noticed the lump. I didn't want to be sick then, David needed me. But I had this crazy feeling that I was going to have to die when he died."

"You liked that?"

"What a pig you are." She put her face in his neck, kissed the folded bristly skin, sucked the layers of sweat and whisky, bit. Christopher leapt, but as his body bounced up from the mattress she rolled on top of him. David was such a stick. Riding on Christopher's belly was like trying to straddle a porpoise. "I like you fat. Promise me not to go on a diet."

"Pervert."

"When they were about to put me under for the operation, David cried. Made me promise to come back. He was afraid I wanted to die. That frightened me because it made me realize I *was* indifferent. Or was pretending to be. Then I woke up and they said they'd got it all. I didn't really believe them but—for the moment—" For the moment Christopher had wrapped his arms around her and she was lying against him.

"Something has happened," she said.

"You feel—"

She was crying, not sobbing but just leaking tears, inside and out. "I have to be with you," she managed to say, knowing it was absolutely true; she *had* to be with Christopher now, would die without him—had to be with him in this body, this room, this night.

"Is it going to have a happy ending?" She couldn't believe her own words, the way her little girl's voice broke as she said them.

Christopher was sitting up now. Christopher, love her? No, surely not—surely when daylight came he would be the same old Christopher—distant, abrasive, ready to use, to twist, to avoid. "He's not a Jew," Bronski had said once, at the camp, by way of explanation of Christopher when he had infuriated her over something she could no longer remember. "Not a Jew? What's the difference? He's *here*, isn't he?" "Yes, he's here. But with him it's an accident. With us—" "With us what?" "With us, because we are Jews, we are sentenced to death." "But everyone is sentenced to death." What happened next she didn't see coming: Bronski hit her, his hand a thunderclap against her ear, knocking her head-first into the concrete wall. No one seemed to find it extraordinary that a young girl was lying in the dirt, bleeding and crying. The next day he greeted her as if nothing had happened. She had a choice, she understood: either accept the lesson, and Bronski, or move out from the umbrella of his protection.

So they had escaped. Or they had not. And so she would escape dying from this cancer. Or she would not. If only she could be with Christopher, *this* Christopher, in *this* stillness; or perhaps even this couldn't work for her. She was holding Christopher's hands—or he was holding hers—they were playing with each other's fingers, turning each other's hands in and out in a strange complicity—just that afternoon, in the supermarket, she had seen two teenagers playing with each other's hands this way, folding and unfolding over the handle of a shopping cart—the boy weak-faced with reddish hair already receding; the girl strangely soft around the mouth, freckled, smiling with such child-like milk teeth that Melanie had wanted to rush over to them, warn that they must *seize* their lives.

She closed her eyes. Christopher was stroking her. She wasn't aroused, but she was soothed. The bad thoughts began to dissolve, break up, float away like unwanted dreams. Christopher's large hands were running over her body. Warm, soothing, a perpetually moving blanket of forgiveness. She was almost asleep; so sleepy she hardly knew if she was feeling Christopher or remembering him.

Jakob was sitting in the straw beside Juliet. Her head moved towards him again, this time gently; her tongue reached out and began methodically working the salt from his opened hands.

When the cow had finished and moved her head away, Jakob reached into his pocket for his cigarettes, tapped one free, lit it with a match he put carefully back in his pocket after blowing it out.

As he smoked he cradled his rifle on his knees, picking it clean of straw. Once, hunting with the director, he had shot a deer at fifty paces. Even from that distance he had seen the deer's head jolt with the force of the bullet. Then, after a brief attempt to shake it off, as though it were a bad dream, the deer had sunk into the snow. Jakob placed the rifle's muzzle against Juliet's head. She stirred slightly, settled back.

At Drancy, when he had realized what he had done to his wife and daughter, he had considered suicide. Why not? For thousands of years Jews trapped in certain situations had chosen death. In order, if nothing else, to deny others the pleasure

of killing. At Drancy he had thought of killing himself, although there were no rifles to make it easy. But then he had
decided—false pride—that if he died it would be in the act of
resisting. Except that when the moment finally came, a guard
had dismissed him with a kick in the face.

Now he had a rifle. Before the mental hospital he had never
even held one. It was the director, wanting a hunting compan-
ion, who started him on target practice. "My tame Jew," the
director called him once. That day they had been in the woods,
alone. How easy it would have been to blow the director's face
into— But that night he and Anna were to meet in Dr. Lydia's
closet. And later Jakob had to admit to himself that the director
had understood him correctly: he had passed the point of being
able to kill.

The cow was sleeping, occasionally twitching her hide to
send away the flies. The muzzle of the rifle had slid down to rest
in her ear. Jakob knelt beside her. He remembered once kneeling
beside Melanie this way, watching her sleep, remembering in
turn the way one night he had watched the sleep of Gabrielle
and Nadine. The infant's head lay between her mother's breasts,
as she slept she sucked on the button of Gabrielle's dressing
gown. He felt proud to watch over his sleeping family, the
small package of flesh contentedly drooling and the half-smile
of motherhood on the face of this beautiful and innocent woman
whose life at that moment—but not only that moment—seemed
to have been placed in his insufficient hands. Watching them,
he swore he would somehow find a way to protect them—cost
what it might. Watching Melanie he had known all his efforts
would be useless. Anna he had never seen sleep. Jakob shifted
the rifle. The cow was breathing hard, its moist black nostrils
shuddering with the rhythm of the night.

Jakob put the rifle in the straw. Then he pulled the letter from
his pocket, ran the tips of his fingers over the paper, smelled it,
cradled it between his palms as though it might conjure up the
image of his daughter.

After the poems had been published he had tried one more piece. Like the poems, he had started it without paper. With them, he had revised and repeated over and over until they found a final form in his memory. Then, in the director's office, while he was supposed to be translating, he simply typed them out. A few minutes for each poem: the whole small book had demanded only a few hours of contraband time at the machine. The thing that he tried to write after, tried to form in his mind, never stayed still long enough for him to type it out. Working in the barn, scrubbing Anna's blood from the steps, lying sleepless in his bed at night, he tried again and again to find the right words for his letter to the dead soul of his daughter. To explain why he had first burned so much to have her, then burned equally to bury it all, offer up his past to Anna for a quick one in the stairway or less. But how to explain to a dead daughter's soul that her father came to believe that, even in the inferno, the most important thing was to turn his back on the past by making love in the cupboards and barns of a mental institution for model patients? How to explain that her father—no youth, no Adonis, no Don Juan, no Jakob conjugating with his angel—suddenly became eager to pull down his pants with a madwoman? How to explain that even after her death, after desire and the memory of desire had passed, he considered those moments the only absolutely forgivable moments of his life?

Jakob climbed out of the stall and walked to the front door of the barn. He pushed it open. A pale rim of light surrounded the horizon.

He lit a cigarette. If his daughter was like everyone else here, she would try to make him stop smoking. That would be something to report to Zev. Easier to believe Comrade Bronski's family would reappear from the grave than to imagine him giving up his daily ration of cigarettes.

By the time he had finished his cigarette and started another, the sky had begun to glow. He was sitting on a hill outside the barn, smoking, the rifle at his feet, when he heard voices coming from the loft across the yard. Christopher's and Melanie's, he recognized them right away, the half-murmur they always used to talk in at Drancy, one voice overlapping the other.

He was listening to them, smoking, contented, when he heard the door of the house slam. David emerged, wearing pyjamas and robe, walking quickly towards the loft. A handsome man, Jakob noted.

He watched David pause below the window, listening to the voices. Then Jakob saw him bend down and select a large rock from the border of the flowerbed.

Without thinking Jakob picked up the rifle, balanced it in his hands as he watched David swing his arm back, then lob the rock through the loft window.

There was the sound of breaking glass. Melanie screamed.

By the time Christopher had emerged through the door, David had his hand around another rock. Melanie, leaning through the broken window, was still screaming.

Jakob swung the rifle into position.

David moved to meet Christopher.

Jakob squeezed the trigger. The explosion in the small valley. The rising sun. The ludicrous sound of cattle bellowing into the new light.

**V**

## 1. Waiting

We are waiting, my mother and I. She is waiting for my father to die, I am waiting for the nurse to tell me that he is ready to be seen. My mother's lips are pressed together, her mouth a constantly shifting rollercoaster of emotions it is my job to decipher. Her eyes are swollen and red, but if she's been crying it's been silently and alone.

We are sitting in a little nook reserved for relatives of patients in intensive care. At the moment we're the only ones, but a few minutes ago there was a priest beside us. He was waiting to see the only other patient in intensive care today, a fellow priest who woke up in the middle of the night, slipped on his way to the bathroom, then began screaming obscenities as the blood seeped into his brain.

About this my mother has made her predictable comments. As well as following with a few obscenities of her own after my father, Professor Doctor David Winters, told her he didn't wish to see her again. In this hospital. In this lifetime.

For the past hour my mother has been flipping through *People*. "Bitch," she said, pointing to one actress. "Do you know she's my age? Face lifts, false tits, dyed hair. Do you think I should look like that?"

Christopher has returned to Paris. "I'd better be alone with him when he dies," my mother explained.

But my father hasn't died yet. From the shopping bag beside her my mother now extracts balls of yarn, needles. At one of her hospitals they taught her how to knit and she made me a huge sweater with a deformed maple leaf on the front. Now she has started knitting again. In the days since my father has been in intensive care she has fashioned a large formless shape. "His shroud," she said yesterday. "As soon as the bastard dies I'm going to run in there and wrap it around him."

Now she raises her eyes from her knitting, looks at me as though I am a stranger in a bus terminal.

"You know," my mother says, "I sometimes wonder what you make of things."

"Make of things?"

Last night it rained but today the sky is blue and summery again. In the strong light my mother's hands look old for the first time. For the first time, also, I am beginning to believe that she may be getting better, that the time may arrive when she no longer needs me.

"What you think, Benjamin. What you make of things. How it all adds up for you. Benjamin, what are you going to do?"

My mother has put down her knitting. I wait for her to continue.

"Benjamin, what are you going to do with your life?"

With my mother and her questions, the trick is simply to wait. Eventually she will start again, ask something else, drift off on a completely different course.

"Are you going to live it with Julia Delfasco? You're doing a job on her, aren't you, Benjamin? Is it supposed to be a secret? The phone calls you make when no one is listening, the way you watched her whenever she was around? You're just like your father, aren't you, Benjamin?"

Then she does something that's not in the script. She sets down her knitting, stands up, comes around to sit beside me.

She has her hands on my cheeks. Her face is closer to mine than it's been for thirty years. I can smell the toast on her breath, the cigarette she stubbed out at the hospital door. Her eyes are bloodshot, the skin around them slowly collapsing. "Poor boy, it's killing you." And still, she doesn't let go. Her face is so close her nose is touching mine. "You're a good boy, Benjamin. You were always a good boy." Now the tears are making lakes in her makeup, her nails are digging into my cheeks.

When the nurse finally rescues me, my mother is the first to move. She kisses me on the mouth, not exactly benediction or forgiveness or even release — a kiss that, like everything else, is mine to decipher.

A few nights ago, before those tears she may or may not have cried, before Christopher left or my father was brought to the hospital—a few nights ago, after the dancing but while lights still shone through the bedroom windows, I had decided to walk down to the lake.

It was some hour after midnight, a time I would not be able, even in court, to identify. The air had cooled and the path leading down to the dock was damp and cold under my bare feet.

The night water was blanketed in the reflections of moon and stars.

I was looking down at myself, the funny way one knee was slightly twisted, my feet, which for reasons unknown have gone their separate ways — one wide and slightly splayed, the other long and narrow. I jumped. Layers of water, growing colder towards the bottom. Soon I was far enough from shore that I could twist and look at the whole bay. I could see the jagged outlines of maple and pine, the faint winking of house lights through the trees. I was thinking about the three of them—Christopher, Jakob, my mother—having their reunion while my father looked on. I was thinking that had he been younger or more sociable, or even if I had just crossed the uncrossable breach, he, too, would have liked to be in the water, feeling the slippery waves on his skin and swimming to the rhythm of frogs grunting in the marsh.

When I got back to the house, Helen was sitting at her worktable, papers spread out in front of her. This past year she had let her hair grow again; now it made a veil around her shoulders, the way it used to when we met.

She turned, and before I could move away her hand came up to take mine.

It must have been just before dawn when I was woken up by Timmy trying to climb into our bed. I took him back to his room.

"Daddy, I can't sleep when my stomach hurts."

"Does your stomach hurt?"

"Daddy, am I God?"

"No."

"I want to be God."

"I know." Timmy was covered in a thin layer of sweat. Even his pillow was wet. I turned it over, then gave him a drink of water and some aspirins.

"I don't like that medicine."

"It makes you better."

"Will I be better in the morning?"

"I hope so."

"Do you promise?"

"I promise."

When I got back to bed Helen was awake.

"How is he?"

"He wants to be God."

"Benjamin Bear," Helen said, the way she used to when she wanted to make love. We were lying on the bed I had built, a bed set on a floor surfaced with tongue-and-groove pine I had spent two fall afternoons sawing and nailing into place.

"You're drifting," Helen whispered. Her hands were moving over me. If I make love with her now, I threatened myself, if I make love with her now, even Uncle Sigmund can't help me.

Only to find myself, not exactly dreaming, lying on top of Helen, bits of fire circling in my body. Not, alas, the fire of desire, as Levin used to call it, but the sparks wires make when they've been rubbed raw. Her hands were on my back, pulling me closer.

But there was nowhere closer to be. I was pumping away for the benefit of my legal wife but all we were doing was finding out what we already should have known, that sex couldn't erase anything—except briefly—and that chief among those events our sex together could not erase was my desire for Julia.

I was just falling asleep again, my eyes half open, when I heard the sound of my mother screaming. I was out of the bed and into my jeans before it stopped.

As I came outside I saw them standing in front of the old horsebarn. My father had a rock in his hand, Melanie was leaning out the window. I started running. Christopher was in front of my father and my father was swinging a rock towards his head. At some time—ten, fifteen years ago—I could still have crossed that gap, sprinted to his rescue before anything bad happened. Saved my father, if only from himself.

But before I could get there, even before the rock filling my father's hand could crush the skull of our guest, came the rifle shot.

In one motion my father turned and fell.

I hadn't seen Bronski but now, rifle in hand, he was walking towards us. My father's eyes were still open and although I can't recall his doing so, I'm sure he must have given me the signal. The good son, the go-between, I leapt head first; it was a cross-body block; hitting Bronski was like being thrown into a cobblestone wall, but he went down, we both went down, me wrenching the rifle out of his hands, him hammering his fist into the side of my face. One of those stub knuckles driving into my temple knocked me out. But I was twisting as I fell, and had time to pull the rifle away from Bronski's stronger grasp, send it spinning like a cheerleader's baton towards Christopher Lewis, who—knees bent, mouth open, arms outstretched—stood waiting.

## 2. Preparing for Final Exams

My father was moved from intensive care. While my mother inspected *People* and *Maclean's* for more examples of cosmetic surgery, I went in to see him. He was lying in bed with his eyes closed. Plastic tubes ran from a tall green oxygen tank into his nose. Thanks to oxygen, drugs, time, the skin of my father's face was not as grey as it had been the day before.

After the stroke one side had been temporarily paralysed. This time, according to Levin, all the damage was localized in the heart. Nothing serious, as heart attacks requiring surgery go. Nothing to fear but death; however, the prognosis was life.

My father's head moved slightly, his lips parted, he continued to sleep. When he groaned, I moved my chair closer, took his hand. A small hand, amazingly, my own father's hand so small it was almost tiny between mine. I slid my fingers to his wrist. The pulse was strong enough—everything considered. So the old muscle was pumping away. A flutter here and there, but stronger than it had been because by the time the ambulance had made it up to the farm, then back to the hospital, an operating team had already been assembled. Now the plumbing around his heart was repaired and reinforced, the old leaks fixed; with the help of a few drugs, a little oxygen, a chemical removal of stress, the ship of fatherhood was at least temporarily afloat. By now even Levin had come down from Heritage Acres to make sure my father got only the best.

After the stroke, I had also sat by my father's bed, held his hand, continually monitored his pulse. And while he slept I would close my own eyes tightly, trying to will the energy from my body into his, cheerlead the paralysed nerves back to life. Now I found myself with my eyes squeezed shut once more, holding onto my father's hand so tightly that I only gradually became aware that the arm attached to the hand was tugging back.

"I'm not dead yet."

I bent over my father, kissed him on the forehead the way I kissed Timmy waking from a fever.

"Thank you. And could you unhook these little tubes? A man feels like a puppet with so much plastic up his nose. You can put them back if I start to go under. Perfect. And now crank up the bed. I feel as though they've laid me out already. That's better. It's a good thing you went to medical school. I always knew it would be useful someday."

Now the bed was up and Professor Doctor David Winters was sitting almost erect, almost as though in the easy chair in his own living room. And I had backed my chair away so that I was at the regulation distance—our regulation distance—a distance close enough for jibes, cleverly disguised insults, challenges, non-sequiturs, but out of danger for touches, hugs or blows.

"How long have you been here?"

"About an hour."

"That must have been exciting, watching the dead man."

"Levin says you're fine. You seem fine."

"I feel good. I noticed you were clutching at my wrist before. How's my pulse?"

"Perfect, everything considered."

"My son, the doctor." And for the first time he smiled at me. "I'm dying, Benjamin. Today, this week, next week—soon. Don't lie to me. Let's not pretend."

"I'm not pretending. You'd be amazed what the human body can withstand. What your body can withstand. All those years out on the farm must have toughened you up."

My father smiled. If he hadn't smiled, I might have gone on to say that I had seen the charts, that Levin and the surgeon had explained that the attack was a symptom of stress—his own anger as much as a reaction to the shot Bronski had fired into the air—and not of a new fundamental weakness of the heart. "The bastard," Melanie had complained once, "he's a dried-up old stick who's afraid to live. You think fucking his secretary is a sign that he's got balls? I'll tell you something, she's the kind of bitch who doles it out and then one day—BAM!—she slams the door. Better tell the old man to watch out or he'll get his dick pinched."

"Why are you smiling?" my father asked me.

"I was thinking," I said.

"Tell me and I promise not to die until tomorrow."

"The day after."

"Tell me first."

"I was remembering one of Mom's crazy phone calls."

"That's all?"

"She thought you were banging your secretary."

"Banging? That's a good one. What did you tell her?"

"What I knew."

My father was getting a certain look on his face now, an expression that hovered between vulnerable and cruel. I had noticed it first when I was a teenager, after I had taken on—unspoken, unadmitted—the role of his protector. Protecting him at first from the tasks that might exhaust him, then from the pain he might have to experience, finally from Melanie as my father made me—unwilling—accomplice to his various lies.

"And you're the good son. When your father's down and out for the count, there you are. When your mother's twenty-third therapeutic nirvana has just crashed, there you are. The Benjamin. Reliable, considerate, constant. You don't even fool around. Too bad I didn't follow your example." My father's cheeks were dead pale with angry red spots in their centre. I was thinking how sweet it would be to connect with my father, really connect. Flesh to flesh, bone to bone. If only he had given me the excuse, some time when he wasn't lying in bed or otherwise incapacitated. But he was lying in bed and he was incapacitated. Even as the red spots on his cheeks began to glow, the tension eased. Then he smiled, subsided, slid back into sleep before I could find the right thing to say. Leaving me to reflect upon our mutual sins, upon the fact that soon I would be in charge of the balance sheet.

That night I dreamed about my father, my father in better days: slim, muscular, fit, wearing jeans stained from the tarring of fence posts. Blue jays and woodpeckers lacing through the cold sky. Through the naked branches of the maple trees, the sun shines a dry fierce yellow. I am with him. On the ground a thin scattering of icy snow. At our feet, chainsaws, axes, wedges.

My father picks up his axe, swings smoothly down into a block of maple. The frozen wood cracks loudly. Satisfied, he stands and rubs his fists into the sore muscles of his back. Jakob appears from behind a tree, effortlessly hoists one of the heaviest logs onto his shoulders, crunches across the snow and throws the log into the back of the pickup truck with a loud clang.

David stares at Jakob as he marches back and forth from woodpile to truck. "His face looks darker," David says. "How long has he been here now?"

"All winter," I answer. In this dream I am larger than life, my father's reliable foot soldier patrolling the borders of the future.

We are in the forest, cutting wood. My mother is back at the house, sitting at the kitchen table surrounded by hundreds of letters, documents, testimonies, photographs of wrongdoing. My father picks up his axe again. Slides the shaft in his hand until he can feel the balance of it running through his arm.

"Death," my father pontificates. "Killing, death, evil. Doesn't it drive you crazy? Do you really want to know everything that goes on? Can you really stand to spend your whole life listening to them— "

Jakob appears beside us. He is smiling. "Forget about good and evil. The truth is all that matters."

My father shakes his head. "When did he learn how to talk?" He rubs his feet in the snow, then takes off a glove and reaches into his jacket pocket for cigarettes. Jakob is staring at him. He wants more, wants debate. But I can see the word "truth" is already sticking in my father's mind, unwanted. "Truth"—hasn't he said it hundreds of times?—"truth is what amateurs believe in." The myth of truth is one of his favourite lectures, one that explains why, at least in history, there is no truth.

Nor is there history. There is no shiny lump of gold, only a compromise working model, a gigantic gizmo patched together out of available evidence—and assembled by whatever rules are acceptable at the moment.

My father offers his cigarettes to Jakob, who moves in closer. In my dream, Jakob glows through his eyes, black glittering eyes encased by massive cheekbones.

"What would be perfect?" my father asks. In this dream, at this moment, my father means to be the perfect host—his home, his land, his cigarettes, his universe—

"A match," Jakob replies.

Explosion of sulphur in the dry air. First drag sharp and acrid.

"Freedom," Jakob announces. "Freedom, liberty, life."

He speaks the words in a low voice. As though we were in Siberia, stamping our feet on the frozen ground of a labour camp. As though we were surrounded by guards who amuse themselves by following our bobbing heads through the sights of their rifles.

"You want a revolution," my father says. "Revolutions are perfect. It's only the people who ruin them."

Jakob explodes with laughter, claps David on the shoulder. "Revisionist! Revisionist!"

I look up at the sky. Pale wintry blue. Clouds turning grey and yellow as the sun slides into the hills. We put our gloves back on, start walking towards the truck. I listen to my feet in the snow. Little moments of eternity.

Then my gloved hands are gripped tightly around the wheel, hanging on as the truck bounces over the frozen rutted road. Sitting beside me is my father; in the open back, astride the cut logs, Jakob is singing loudly. "I don't know what can happen," my father says. He is looking at me, at my face, at the scar—now a fine white line—that drifts down from the corner of my left eye. My father was watching me when that happened. Midget hockey, a stick carelessly swung, blood sheeting down my face as I fell. And even while I was trying to feel for my eye, I could hear my father clumping across the ice in his galoshes, calling my name.

The road twists. The landscape shifts. Instead of my going back through the village as I meant to, something is leading me deeper into the bush. The setting sun has turned the cold blue winter sky into a spectacular dome of flames. The road is so narrow that trees are scratching against the doors of the truck. Somehow Jakob has climbed into the cab. The small space is thick with the smells of grease and sweat and sawdust. The truck skids off the road and drifts harmlessly into a snowbank.

"Here we are," Jakob says.

Now he leads the way as we walk through the snow. We are carrying rifles. I notice that my father's sweating face looks sallow and unhealthy. When Jakob stops, my father is breathing hard. Otherwise, absolute silence.

"We're here," Jakob says. We know what he means. He means that we have arrived at our destination, at the centre of the dream we have been dreaming together. Soon something will be revealed: a mass grave, an armed camp, a naked woman, an orchestra playing Mozart. The details don't matter. Or, on the other hand, perhaps the details are the whole point. Jakob, we now know—my father and I—is going to show us something awful. That is why he is here. My job is to be the witness. My father's job is to die.

## 3. Wearing the Clothes of the Dead Man

My father died at the end of September, after two months in hospital—first in Kingston, then Toronto. Two months of getting neither better nor worse. Two months of patiently waiting to die, of—I eventually realized—doing nothing more than breathe and watch his life grow transparent and slip away. The official line was that he was getting better, that his heart was healing and repairing itself.

He died early one morning. It was totally unexpected; Ruth was in Vancouver researching a travel article for her magazine.

I was the one who shed the tears. Melanie just stared at him. In death he looked himself: well-barbered grey hair, face composed and closed, hands neatly laced together. I couldn't keep myself, crying, from kneeling beside him, kissing his hands. When I stood up Melanie was waiting at the door.

She was composed, rock-hard. If she hadn't needed to hold onto my arm while we walked down the corridor, I would have thought she was totally untouched.

"I'm going to call Christopher," she announced when we got home.

"Will he come to the funeral?"

"I don't want him to. I don't want to see him until this is over.

That afternoon, while the others watched over my mother, Levin and I went to choose the coffin at the funeral parlour. For the occasion, Levin dressed in a white lab coat and a stethoscope. "It drives them crazy," he assured me.

The salesman had badly bitten nails—to hide them he kept sticking his fists into his pockets.

"We want something secure," Levin instructed.

Now the pockets jerked. "Something of ... high quality?"

"I want it to look like Fort Knox," Levin said. "You know, solid. We don't want the family having nightmares about him escaping, do we?"

"Of course not, sir." The man's face was sandpapery and pocked, as though he himself might have been resurrected not so long ago. Through the speakers came reassuring music played by an orchestra of ten thousand strings. "We have this stainless steel model, sir."

"Guaranteed?" asked Levin. He began fiddling with his stethoscope, then lifted it up and placed the cup on the salesman's tie. "When did you last have a checkup?"

"Perhaps I should try to see if the manager is available, sir."

As soon as the salesman was gone, Levin began pacing the room, peering inside the various coffins, punching their padding as though they were car tires, tapping the shiny trim with his nails.

"Take this," Levin said.

I turned around. Levin was lying in one of the coffins, smoking a cigarette and holding out a match.

"For Christ's sake, Levin, what if the manager catches you?"

"I was just trying it," Levin said. "If he thinks I've stained it or something we'll buy it. Now take this match before it ruins the upholstery. Didn't your mother teach you manners?"

Levin, skinny and gnome-like, wiggled comfortably in the satin cushioning and puffed smoke rings. "Your mother tells me you're fucking Julia Delfasco."

"I was."

"Pure sex."

"You say."

"When I was a kid I would have liked to fuck Julia Delfasco."

"When you were a kid you would have liked to fuck sheep, brother-in-law."

"So why did you stop?"

"For Christ's sake, Levin, I'm a married man."

"So why did you start?"

"Levin, if they catch you in there you'll get sent to jail for necrophilia."

"I'm not that excited. But tell me, Dr. Winters, why *did* you start fucking Julia Delfasco? Aside from the obvious. And if it was so great, why did you stop?"

"Who said it was so great?"

"Dr. Winters, let me remind you that you're speaking of a trusted employee who, in addition to providing a home to your stray desires, has also contributed to the well-being of your mother."

"Is she upset?"

"Dr. Winters, you are the one who is upset. You are the one who—"

What he said next, I don't know. But I do remember reaching into the coffin, grabbing Laurence Levin by his lab coat and hauling him out. "You asshole!" I screamed. I was holding him in the air, watching his feet kick helplessly. Levin, my father, my mother, Julia, Helen, Timmy—why did my whole world have to be filled with these helpless pink bunnies? "Weakling bastard!" I shouted in his face. Levin buried his knee in my gut. Even when I hit him back he kept fighting.

Later that afternoon Levin told my mother we had got into a fight with some strangers over a parking space at the liquor store.

The funeral was larger than expected. Not only did my father's former students and colleagues from the university come, but also a huge contingent from the Toronto Jewish community. Their motive, it seemed from the cranings of necks and whisperings, was the first public appearance of the refugee himself.

Broad, gnarled, his face twisted into itself, his rediscovered daughter clinging to his arm, Bronski stood motionless and mute throughout the service. Afterwards, I noticed that Bronski stopped and was courteously replying to questions. Then he rejoined us. His face, when he looked at his daughter, seemed strangely naked and vulnerable.

"He's in love again," Melanie said when we were alone in the car. "Ruth and your father were like that. Or would have been, if your father had let her. Isn't it disgusting the way daughters can love their fathers? It's the only reason I would have wanted to be a man."

And then she leaned forward and took one of my hands. "I know you've tried, Benjamin. I appreciate it." And then: "Are you still going to bed with Julia Delfasco?"

"No."

"I suppose you'll be just like your father."

"He wasn't that bad."

"He wasn't that bad," Melanie mimicked. "How bad would he have had to be?"

"You weren't the only one he hurt."

My mother was crying. Good. I wanted her to cry. Louder, harder, whatever it would take to balance the thousands of hours I had poured into her unsalvable wounds, her inexhaustible complaints, her endless and pointless decades of mourning.

"Maybe he only wanted to marry you, not six million dead Jews—"

And saying it, I suddenly knew it was true. My father the history professor, Doctor Professor David Winters, had only been an innocent, a man like other men, like me, a cocky lonely vulnerable ambitious middle-aged creature stranded in the middle of a life he didn't understand, suddenly confronted with the possibility of escaping into a universe of soft skin, warm arms.

"You know what? I feel sorry for your father. He was an asshole but he died for nothing. Bring the patient back to reality. That's always the first rule. But no one was crying, you have to admit. Even Jakob kept his eyes dry. You'd think he'd at least have felt sorry for murdering him."

"He didn't murder him. As you know. And people were crying. Even you were crying."

"Maybe I was. The crazy thing is I couldn't help feeling sorry for him. Poor little guy, I kept thinking, poor little dead guy. He was so old, so out of fashion, he lived his whole life in a little box and then he got buried in it. All things considered, how can I begrudge him poking his little lance around looking for some excitement? It was all he could come up with."

Now the poor little guy was in a padded box, guaranteed ten years, six feet under as they used to say, safe from the frost and my mother's tongue.

*4. My Mother's Hands*

My mother's hands. Long fingers tipped with manicured nails that float on her skin like the moons of a faraway planet.

On the table between us is the VICTIMS & PRISONERS file, and on top of the file a letter from Christopher Lewis.

It is December, afternoon. Five months since that afternoon last summer when I sat with her at Heritage Acres, when I argued with Norton Meredith about whether or not she could survive in the house where she now lives. The letter in question, that afternoon, was the one from Jakob Bronski. That afternoon, despite what I had said to Meredith, I didn't really believe in Bronski's powers, didn't really see how he could make a difference. Now, in a few minutes, we will be joined by the man himself. In black wool coat, fur hat, carrying a cane, he makes his way on foot through the snowy Toronto streets. He will bring his own packets of letters, his strong-smelling French cigarettes, the strange peaceful glow that the last few months have drawn from him.

"Christopher's coming here for Christmas," my mother announces. "A long visit. He says I may never get rid of him." These days she is surrounded by men: myself, as always; Bronski, who sees her almost every afternoon; Levin, who comes with Ruth for dinner several times a week; Christopher, who sends her books and letters; and of course Timmy—Timmy, who dotes on her, demands his daily ration of card-playing from her, needs to be kissed by her at night and woken by her in the morning.

"If only he'd been born twenty years ago, he could have kept me out of the nuthouse," Melanie says.

It would be convenient to be able to say that for the moment everything is wrapped up, the equations balanced, the debts if not paid at least acknowledged. But as Levin said when I finally talked to him about Julia: "Am I supposed to congratulate you or remind you what an idiot you are?"

Bronski is at the door. He comes inside kicking snow from his boots and shaking his heavy wool coat. His cheeks are pink, his eyes bright. Beneath his sports jacket, a new tweed number forced on him by his daughter, he wears a ragged maroon sweater knitted, he says, by a woman he knew in the hospital. These last months he seems to have grown even larger. And since our collision in the barnyard we always shake hands with the utmost care, like two old athletes who once fought each other and now, friends, can't believe they risked life and limb. "People like us," he often says to my mother, "we terrify them." In Bronski's war of the worlds it's the nuts versus the dictators, and my mother knows what he means.

Meanwhile Bronski and my mother are drinking tea and shuffling their papers. Soon letters will be written, phone calls made, old voices that won't die will buzz through the ether.

My mother's hands. Long fingers waving to Timmy and me as we set off across the lawn. My mother, Christopher and Jakob are sitting beneath the big maple tree near the house. When I was Timmy's age I helped my father prune that tree, stood on a stepladder while he showed me how to fill the scars with thick black tar.

It is a year since my father had his final heart attack. My mother, Christopher and Jakob have come up to the farm to visit us. To remember, my mother says—pretending she means my father's death—but the truth is that something inside her needs another taste of that first reunion, of that night she became herself again.

As we get into the boat Timmy insists on taking the oars. He's bigger this summer, the future is pulling at his bones. As he rows us out from the shore he grins at me, gap-toothed. I, too, have been tugged by the future. Next month I return to medical school. With the plan of specializing in psychiatry and, as Levin calls it, "joining the M.D., the Ministry of Desire."

Levin also insists that after I get my certificates we will have to go into business: together with some cosmetic surgeons, he has suggested, we will establish the Church of Perfection on the farm. The barns will be used as dormitories for the patient-aspirants, and Levin, as personnel manager, will hire a squadron of large-chested men and women to work for us.

"You're disgusting," I tell him.

He protests: "If it weren't for you, I'd still have Julia."

This may be true. Anyway, Julia has been promoted from my unreliable arms to those of Norton Meredith's rich and adoring accountant. When she quit work she told Levin he was "a voyeuristic pig and don't even ask me about your friend."

Timmy has taken us out of the bay and is heading towards a reedy patch across the lake. He is wearing a lifejacket; sticking out from the blocky padded vest his pipestem arms look even thinner than usual.

While Timmy rows I fasten the lures to the fishing-lines. The sky is a milky blue, humid, and cloud is beginning to settle around the horizon. It's a hot day. We're both wearing hats, Timmy and I, round straw numbers I found at the supermarket.

On the other side of the lake is a long piny beach owned by some Americans from Rochester. Now they've put up a fancy all-weather chalet with a panel of black glass in the roof so the sun will heat their water. Thinking of this I remind myself of my father, always remembering how things were before such-and-such was built, burned down, transformed. As if the present were nothing more than a temporary mistake laid on top of reality—the past. But that chalet *is* a mistake. Fifteen years ago it wasn't even there. That ugly clearing in the pines was a small meadow. I would row girlfriends across the lake to the Americans' land and we would take off our clothes and lie in the soft beds of needles. When we were finished I would dive into the lake, rolling around in the clean water until the needles were gone and my skin was new again.

Where will Timmy take his girlfriends? Will I tell him how pure and clean I felt as the water lifted away the pine needles and sent them floating into oblivion?

Now Timmy has stopped rowing. He takes his fishing rod, the child-sized one with the red and green plastic popping frog, and holds it upright. Expertly, as though not last month but fifty years ago I showed him how, he sets the tip quivering. Then, with a quick flick of the wrist, sends the lure arcing towards the reeds. A soft plop and it's snugly in place, right in their midst.

He looks at me. "Perfect," I say. "People go to school to learn how to cast like that."

"Be quiet, Daddy." But as he begins drawing the lure home Timmy is grinning to himself, repeating the words. When the fish strikes, his first, he is so surprised that the rod jumps in his hands. He hangs on; then jerks back the rod to set the hook. The fish, a trout, breaks the surface, its long dripping body a perfect rainbow magically suspended above the lake. Then it's under again and Timmy's rod bends double as he struggles to bring it in. I'm watching, but for me the real action is Timmy's face— amazed, fierce, terrified; my son is locked in a battle he doesn't understand but needs to win.

When the trout is finally at the boat I grab the line, scoop the fish out of the water and into a bucket where it continues to twist and leap.

"Will you take the hook out?"

"This time. You watch me." The trout is long and sleek. Silky skin. Faint stripes blushing with colour running from gills to tail. The mouth working in the air. I hold it behind the gills, force the hook backwards out of the trout's lip. Timmy leans close. Extends his hand. Runs a cautious finger along the curving flesh.

"Give it to me."

He takes the fish, wraps his small hands around its squirming body. His eyes are pushed together, his mouth screwed up, tears leaking down his cheeks. And then suddenly he's leaning over the side of the boat and the trout has slid from his hands into the water.

A flick of the tail and, except for a small whip of blood wrapped around the plastic frog, it is gone.

When we get back to the house they're still sitting outside, drinking tea and sorting through my mother's files. Timmy runs to tell her about his adventure. The three old heads turn towards him. They're in their own world, their own sealed dream, one I finally know will always be closed to me. As the words gush out of Timmy they peer curiously. Smile. Reach out to touch.